GATHERINGS

The En'owkin Journal of First North American Peoples

VOLUME III

MOTHER EARTH PERSPECTIVES:

PRESERVATION THROUGH WORDS

Fall, 1992

Theytus Books, Penticton, British Columbia

GATHERINGS:
The En'owkin Journal of First North American Peoples

Volume III - 1992

Published annually by Theytus Books Ltd. for the En'owkin Centre International School of Writing

Managing Editor:	Greg Young-Ing
Associate Editors:	Jeannette Armstrong, Gerry Williams, Tracey Kim Bonneau, Don Fiddler
Guest Editorial:	Dr. David Suzuki
Page Composition:	Banjo, Linda Squakin, Tracey Kim Bonneau, Regina Gabriel
Proofreading:	Alice Rix, Lil Sheps, Anna Kruger
Cover Design:	Greg Young-Ing, Banjo
Cover Art:	Simon Paul Dene (Original painting entitled "Mother Tongue")

A catalogue will be mailed upon request.

Please inquire about our advertising rates and contributors' guidelines.

Please send submissions and letters to 'Gatherings', c/o En'owkin Centre, 257 Brunswick Street, Penticton, B.C. V2A 5P9 Canada. All submissions must be accompanied by self-addressed stamped envelope (SASE). Manuscripts without SASEs may not be returned. We will not consider previously published manuscripts or visual art.

Typeset by Theytus Books Ltd. Printed and bound in Canada

ISSN 1180-0666
ISBN 0-919441-42-4

TABLE OF CONTENTS

Section III - SUMMER

Section V - KIDS

Section VI - GUESTS (International Indigenous)

Section VII - ELDERS

Editorial

Once again, on behalf of **The En'owkin International School of Writing, Theytus Books** and **The En'owkin Centre** are proud to present another volume of "Gatherings: The En'owkin Journal of First North American Peoples". **Gatherings** is the only journal of writing by First Nation authors in North America and is published annually by Theytus Books - a First Nations owned and operated publishing house.

This past summer a historical event took place at the University of Oklahoma when over two hundred writers gathered for *"Returning the Gift: A Festival of North American Native Writers"*. It was an invigorating experience to witness the majority of First Nations writers in North America gathered together in one spot. Those of us who attended from The En'owkin Centre received both encouragement from several participants to continue our work and overwhelming support for the "Gatherings" journal. For us, this alone makes the incredible amount of work we put into compiling, editing, producing and publishing the journal each year seem worthwhile.

The theme of this third volume of Gatherings is **"Mother Earth Perspectives: Preservation Through Words"**. Through this theme, we have put together a diverse selection of work featuring First Nations people from across North America expressing reverence, love and concern for Our Land and all of the Natural World - a compassion which is, of course, deeply rooted in our cultures and world views.

One of the things that has given me the greatest pride in my First Nations heritage are the ideological principles and appropriate technological systems developed by our ancestors - highly complex systems which adhere to the principle of sustainable development and take into account all aspects of life. Our Elders have always taught us that the Creator placed us in our territories and clearly set out our responsibility as caretakers. The extent to which First Nations were successful in developing ways of life in tune with the natural balance of Creation is evidenced by the fact that there was a total lack of pollution, environmental deterioration and endangered or extinct species due to unnatural phenomenon, before European penetration of the Continent.

Please enjoy the variety of writing contained the following pages and experience the enlightening perspectives of First Nation peoples on our environment and forging paths to lead us out of our current ecological crisis.

ALL MY RELATIONS,

Greg Young-Ing,
Editor

Dr. David Suzuki

Guest Editorial

In the remaining years of this century, we must escape the ecologically destructive path we are on and begin to live in balance with the productive carrying capacity of the Earth.

The list of environmental dangers we face are familiar and indisputable: a human population that increases by 3 people a second; a decline in global food production since 1984 through topsoil loss of 25 billion tonnes a year; toxic chemical poisoning of air, water and soil; atmospheric change from acid rain, ozone depletion and accumulation of greenhouse gasses; destruction of tropical rainforest at the rate of one acre per second; species extinction at an estimated rate recently revised up to 50,000 species annually.

Human beings are now the deadliest predator in the history of life on Earth. We have reached this unprecedented state of urgency because we no longer remember that we are animals who retain an absolute need for air, water, soil and other life forms for our survival.

In the 500 years since Columbus' arrival, the waves of immigrants to North America have lacked the respect for the Earth as a sacred place and the spiritual connection to the land that the Aboriginal people have. To the newcomers, land and its resources were merely "commodities", or "opportunities" to be exploited until exhausted and then abandoned. Today, transnational companies with head offices in other countries with even less attachment to the land, continue to accelerate the destructive process to maximize profit.

If we are to resolve our ecocrisis, we must achieve a new spiritual covenant with the land and with all of the other life forms with whom we share this planet. I have learned from my Aboriginal friends in Canada, the U.S.A., Brazil, Sarawak, and Australia, that they understand to the very core of their being that the Earth is their Mother, the source of life itself, and this tinges their actions with respect and reverence. We, non-Aboriginal people, have much to learn spiritually from Aboriginal people and need to do so through dialogue based on mutual respect and dignity.

It would indeed be the greatest achievement to reach the new millennium living in harmony with the planet.

"**Mother Earth Perspectives: Preservation Through Words**", the theme of this third volume of Gatherings: The En'owkin Journal of First North American People, is a calling to incorporate the Aboriginal voice in the effort to save our future. In the following pages you will read Aboriginal people expressing concern and respect for their Mother Earth ranging from writings by some of the most highly acclaimed and published Aboriginal authors in North America, to young students attending the En'owkin International School of Writing.

It is high time we learned to listen and allow ourselves to benefit from the teachings and perspectives of Aboriginal people themselves. In the midst of all the misrepresentation, misinformation and propaganda that exits out there, I consider it a blessing that my Aboriginal friends at the En'owkin Centre and Theytus Books have taken on the responsibility of compiling and publishing this important annual journal of writing by Aboriginal people.

Dr. David Suzuki

The David Suzuki Foundation's
DECLARATION OF INTERDEPENDENCE

THIS WE KNOW: We are the earth, through the plants and animals that nourish us. We are the rains and the oceans that flow through our veins. We are the breath of the forests of the land, and the plants of the sea. We are human animals, related to all other life as descendants of the firstborn cell. We share with these kin a common history, written in our genes. We share a common present, filled with uncertainty. And we share a common future, as yet untold.

We humans are but one of thirty million species weaving the thin layer of life enveloping the world. The stability of communities of living things depends upon this diversity. Linked in this web, we are interconnected - using, cleansing, sharing and replenishing the fundamental elements of life. Our home, planet Earth, is finite; all life shares its resources and the energy from the sun, and therefore has limits to growth. For the first time, we have touched those limits. When we compromise the air, the water, the soil, and the variety of life, we steal from the endless future to serve the fleeting present.

We may deny these things, but we cannot change them.

THIS WE BELIEVE: Humans have become so numerous and our tools so powerful that we have driven fellow creatures to extinction, dammed the great rivers, torn down ancient forests, poisoned the earth, rain and wind, and ripped holes in the sky. Our science has brought pain as well as joy; our comfort is paid for by the suffering of millions. We are learning from our mistakes, we are mourning our vanished kin, and we now build a new politic of hope. We respect and uphold the absolute need for clean air, water and soil. We see that economic activities that benefit the few while shrinking the inheritance of many are wrong. And, since environmental degradation erodes biological capital forever, full ecological and social cost must enter all equations of development. We are one brief generation in the long march of time; the future is not ours to erase. So where knowledge is limited, we will remember all those who will walk after us, and err on the side of caution.

THIS WE RESOLVE: All this that we know and believe must now become the foundation of the way we live. At this turning point in our relationship with Earth, we work for an evolution; from dominance to partnership; from fragmentation to connection; from insecurity to interdependence.

WINTER

Today We Will Not Be Invisible

today
we will not be invisible or silent
as the pilgrims of yesterday continue their war of attrition
forever trying, but never succeeding
        in their battle to rid the americas of us
convincing others and ourselves
        that we have been assimilated & eliminated

                but we remember who we are

we are the spirit of endurance that lives
in the cities and reservations of North America
and in the barrios and countryside of Nicaragua, Chile
Guatemala, El Salvador

and in all the earth and rivers of the americas

500 Years And Still Counting

500 years of lightning and storms
500 years of torrents of rain
500 years ago
        thunder tore the skies
shredding clouds into strips of cotton
rain beating down on the land
your hand in mine peaceful and soothing
huddled together against the chill
sheltered by skins and furs, unprepared
for the coming wars
and the drenching of our shores

was the rain only the beginning
        of many years more of deceit and torture?
was the rain only the beginning
        of more storms to come
        500 years (and more) of genocide
disease, lies
        and hate?

500 years
        of fear
afraid to share
        fear
self-centered and greedy
striking out in fear
afraid of the unknown
a people dark,
forests green and home to four-leggeds
mysterious and kind

wolves are not for murder
children, women and men are not to be hunted
500 years and still counting
500 years, how many more deaths will we endure?

Peter A. Ettagiak

The Greatest Polar Bear (Oratory)

This story is about the greatest polar bear in the NorthWest Territories. The scientific name of the northern bear is "Nanook." Nanook is the right word to describe this bear. The polar bear is a fearsome beast.

The strongest and most cunning bear that ever lived and roamed the Arctic in the late 1880's was called Macho. He weighed nearly two tons and he was 11 feet long from tip of nose to tip of tail. He earned his name when he lost three claws from one paw in an escape from a gun shot wound. After that, he was never shot again by a hunter.

Hundreds of hunters tried to kill Macho for nearly thirty years. He roamed free. He feared nothing. It is said that Macho killed a whole dozen of seals and walrus. He crushed the seals' and walrus' spines with his strong jaws.

What Macho could not kill, he would outwit. Again and again he escaped from groups of hunters. Once he led seven hunters through snow-covered icebergs for more than a week. Then he left his pursuers behind. They found out that they were more than 150 miles from home.

Once a hunter made what he thought was a foolproof bear trap. He fastened a heavy spear to an iceberg and hung a piece of raw meat from a cord to the spear. The hunter was sure that Macho would tug at the bait and the spear would fire and kill Macho, but Macho proved his cunning way once more. He came up from behind and pushed aside the point of the spear. When he took the bait, the spear fired into the air instead of at the bear.

Many men have told stories of Macho's courage. A walrus once watched from the safety of a piece of ice as the bear stalked a herd of walrus in the icy weather. He saw Macho choose a calf and brought it down with one blow. The calf's mother tried to rake Macho with her white sharp tusks. But the bear killed her too. Then the herd bull charged. He lifted Macho onto his white tusks and hauled him into the scrub. With a roar of rage, the polar bear came out of the water and rose up on his hind legs and met the mad bull head on as he charged again. Macho wrenched the bull's head to the side and broke the bull's spine with one crunch of his jaws.

No one knows how many walrus, seals, and fishes Macho slaughtered during his life; the number was probably very large. The hunters of the area offered many rewards for his capture. At last, in 1991, he met his match. Two hunters caught sight of Macho across on an ice pack; he was about 125 yards away from them. Both fired their guns and the shots struck home. The polar bear staggered slightly, then he wheeled around and charged. As he lumbered up the ice towards them, the two men pumped shot after shot into him. The raging giant paid no heed to the bullets. He was within thirteen yards of the hunters before he finally stumbled, slumped to the ice, and died. It took ten direct hits, three of them to the head, to bring him down. Finally!

Macho was never forgotten. He was the greatest polar bear of the NorthWest Territories. The greatest of all-time.

Raven Hail

Winter Solstice

The dark Goddess gathers
all Her fallen blossoms
unto the warm earth
to await new birth.

Mary Lawrence

Blanket of Snow

Clouds hanging heavy
        in the depths of winter
Blades of grass still green
        awaiting winter's snow
Oh! How I live to see
        a fresh blanket of snow
With birds that sing
        winter's melody
And all the leaves
        drooping from
Winter's last
        snowy hour

Mary Lawrence

Cruel Years

Riding through rolling hills, valleys and hovering fir and pine trees, we sat restlessly on the bus in the early afternoon. The boarding school was about ninety miles north of our reserve, situated at the head of the Kamloops Indian Reserve. I felt sudden stabs of anxiety as we neared the emerging city of Kamloops. Unlike those beautiful wild flowers crowning the trails back home, dry, yellow, tumbleweeds covered the barren hillsides. I scanned the countryside, squinting and blinking behind the sooty bus window.

We were picked up at the bus station by an aide from the school, driven to the grounds, about one mile north of the city. I suspect it was an aide who picked us up because my memory fails me here. Perhaps I have suppressed this part of my journey because it was too distressing.

Upon arriving, the first thing that caught my drowsy eyes was the oval swimming pool directly in front of the building. I rubbed my eyes and looked at the sparkling blue water and the large red-brick structure. I moved closer to my older sister, Marge, and we stood there mesmerized by our new surroundings.

Marge was then about ten or eleven years old and Hugh was a year younger. I would be turning nine in September.

We stood in front of the large double-doors in the warm afternoon sun waiting to be admitted. A lanky, scrubbed-looking priest opened the door. He wore dark-rimmed glasses and was dressed in a long black tunic. Father Dunlop was greying slightly at the temples and had a receding hairline. He invited us in. Immediately we were separated. Hugh went to the boys dormitory and Marge and I were diverted to a large sleeping room containing many army-like beds. Each bed was neatly made in military fashion. The corners of the sheets were tightly tucked in and one grey wool blanket was folded across the bottom of each bed. The sheets looked spotlessly clean and crispy. Again, my memory fails. I cannot recall the torment I must have felt departing from my pint-sized beloved brother. Before coming here, we lived in a one-room log cabin with two wobbly beds, a table and a pot-belly stove. Marge, Hugh and I all slept in the same bed. We rubbed our feet together during the cold months and grasped at covers to keep warm. I missed that very much.

A year proceeded and I completed grade four. We returned from our reserve after the summer holidays and began another year, (in the same building) with exactly the same regulations.

I liked grade five. Probably because I discovered my puppy-love. I sat behind a boy named Vonnet Hall who had curly dark brown hair and a shy smile. We liked each other but were too bashful to talk to one another. His delicate smiles aroused me and my heart would go pitter-patter. Remarkably, six years later, while he was training at the cadet camp in Vernon we met unexpectedly and started dating. During our stroll to the movies, we joked about our nostalgic feelings towards each other in grade five. Our dating was very brief during those two summer months. I think we both realized puppy-love does not endure forever.

The Oblates of Mary Immaculate disciplined the Indian kids everyday, particularly in the Catholic creed. Sister Leonita's thin, small-framed body emerged from her bedroom at the crack of dawn each morning at 6:30 a.m. She would begin the day by ringing a medium-sized cow bell, pacing rampantly in the dorm, with her other feeble hand sprawling in the air in all directions. She would yell, "Everyone up!" We would tumble out of bed, brush our teeth and quickly put on our starched white blouses with matching navy-blue box-pleated tunics. We would put on our hand-scrubbed white bobby-socks with black oxfords and assemble in the chapel for 7:30 a.m. mass. The pews were uncomfortable and my knees were always sore from frequently kneeling. After mass, we would line up two by two and go to the dining roomwhere we picked up our breakfast trays.

The evening prayers, Benediction, and Sunday mass were as timely as a grandfather pendulum clock. I began to despise this forced feeding of religion. My Catholic upbringing was becoming a burden.

During our second year at the school, my six-year-old brother, Bill, came with us. Although the boys and girls were kept separated, I still managed to squeeze Bill's hand in the hallway and mutter, "Hi, Bill," whenever he passed in single file to their cafeteria. Bill stood out from the other little boys because he was the only one with dirty-blonde hair. He would poke his head out and reach for my hand and squeeze it as he hurried past, cheerfully greeting me with, "Hi, Sis."

One weekend in the late autumn season, Mom came to visit. We walked about a mile into town and spent the afternoon romping in the park, snapping pictures and having fun. Inside Mom's brown shopping bag was her concealed bottle of booze, probably a jug of wine. She preferred red to white wine. During the afternoon, she sneaked gulps from the bottle. By the time we had to return to the school, it was dark and Mom was intoxicated, kept slurring her words. Instead of walking along the highway to the turn-off, we took a short-cut along the river bank. I became fearful, remembering the tall trees, dark woods, and the scary things that I heard at the school about the swamps and quicksand. I carefully watched every step I took in the dark. We arrived safely, yet

I felt cheated one more time. Again, Mom's good intentions were swallowed up by a despicable bottle of booze. I felt embarrassed returning to school with a staggering mother. Despite this, I cannot recall anyone saying anything to us, or for that matter even letting us back in. Mom never came to visit again. Her letters came regularly though - from jail, bearing promises that she would quit drinking when she got out. I always looked forward to Mom's letters even though they came in yellow-lined stationery with the envelope clearly marked "Lower Mainland Correctional Centre." Back in those days, six-month jail sentences were handed down readily to the Indians who were caught under the influence of alcohol. Mom certainly did enjoy sipping wine in the company of others, underneath the evergreen trees in the old Veteran's Memorial Park in Vernon.

Regularly, during this year at Kamloops, I received letters from my Aunt Yvonne. Once she tucked something inside her letter. It was a red-diamond ring with two tiny white stones on each side. I proudly wore my favourite ring until the band got all crooked and my finger changed to a yellowish-green colour.

My best friend, Annie, had short brown hair and big bright eyes. We giggled together and shared our secrets and her foodstuffs. Her family was not poor, so whenever Annie received care packages from home, she would share with me. We were usually in the playground, twirling around on the merry-go-round when Annie would be called to pick up her package. It would be neatly stuffed with packages of candy, fresh oranges, apples and marshmallows. We were seldom provided fresh fruit or sweets, so when Annie shared her goodies, I cherished our friendship. Her gestures of kindness restored a humanness during my ruthless captivity.

In passing the staff kitchen every morning we only caught the whiff of warm buttered toast and the lingering smell of bacon and eggs. For breakfast we faced cold oatmeal porridge. I gagged as I forced the soft, undesirable food down my throat. I have no recollection of what we had for lunch. For supper, usually we were served a syrupy, googly-guck mixture of meat, along with lumpy instant mashed potatoes. I always collected many slices of brown and white bread to substitute the suppers that were unbearable to eat.

After three years of attending the school, coming home only for Christmas and summer holidays, we returned to stay home permanently. I secretly tucked away my feelings toward the ill-natured nuns, the filthy food, and the repetition of prayer. I simply enjoyed living at Grandma's house. Early in the morning, I liked the cracking sound of the kindling in the wood stove just after Grandma put firewood in. I loved the smell of her first pot of coffee brewing. Grandma's bannock tasted so good. Her stories were even better. She always mused about her hard times growing up. Grandma always thought we had it good in Kamloops with three square meals a day, a bed to sleep in every night, and a chance to learn and get a good education. We listened when she talked and dared not ask about the next boarding school.

Tracey Kim Bonneau

KN kn a? xwa'

inca ken sqilx w
I am an Indian

Way' lim limt kwul n' cuten
Thank you Creator for the land

ala' in tmxwulaxw
this is my land

Kn kn a? xwa'

the spirit fish are calling you
they are emerging
from cancerous
death patterns and
spiral designs
that slap white
foam
against the
cold concrete walls of the
Grand Coulee Dam

Kn kn a? xwa' ....

" what.... where am I ??? and who the hell are you.....hey you got a light... I want to light this cigarette here...hey what's with all the dead fish....hey man don't do that....hey man what the *%@! do you think your doing...I said *%@! off.... leave those fish alone ....can't you see ...(puff..puff)....hey stop it!!!!
...(gag)...(wheeze)....listen to me....come on....listen

inca ken squilx w
I am an Indian

Way' lim limt kwul n' cuten
Thank you creator for the land

a la ' in tmwulaxw
THIS IS MY LAND

Kn Kn a? xwa' is the great salmon Chief of the Kettle Fall's area. He was like the fish warden before European contact. He carried two rocks which he would smash together down at the Columbia River and that was the great ceremony which opened the salmon season to all visiting tribes that built encampments along the Columbia River.

Kn Kn a? xwa' is still alive but the Grand Coulee Dam stopped the salmon run.....Kn Kn a? xwa' is my brother. He is alive........ wey ya way ya whey ya ha .....ya whey ya way ya hey way ya whey......wheeeeee

Tracey Kim Bonneau

Sig Em

Tall cottonwood
trees
surrounded
sacred fires
as Liliwat
hearts
echoed in desperation

a whirlwind
of mounties
jerked
sisters and grammas
off an imaginary
line
that was drawn
so carefully
so gently

sixty-four brothers and sisters
coiled inside
rings of a lifeline
embedded in a tree

like fireflies the mounties
painted the sky
with colourful "hell i cop ters"
looking through their
electronic eyelids
waiting....

sixty-four brothers and sisters
singing good medicine
until the mountain awoke
and beamed
into a landslide
that no one understood
except the mocassin telegraph
of sixty-four brothers and sisters

* This poem is dedicated to the Lil'wat peoples movement.

Tracey Kim Bonneau

Nine One One

She had a dream. She got up in the middle of the night and cupped a small amount of water into her wrinkled hand, from the rusted tap. Her eyes were old and torn with sadness. I put on the kettle and asked gramma why she was hurting. She said she had a bad dream. It was no good. She told me about the images that were in her nighmare. It came out in a verse something like this, "You know there are some real nice things that the new people spoiled out here. I look at the lake and I worry about it. That milfoil stuff someone brought out on a boat ...it never used to be here. Now the lake is choking because this stuff ain't supposed to grow here. Then they took this chemical called 2-4-D and said that it would help kill the milfoil. They didn't even think of what it would do to the people or to the lake. Then the people started getting bathrooms in their houses and.... holy cow.... they started putting all their poop into the lake."

I almost choked on my tea. Gramma cut her baking powder biscuit in half and spread some chokecherry and elder berry jelly on it; she looked at me hard into the eyes and said, "We mustn't be blaming these people even though they brought a bunch of bad things over, they also brought some good things too. They have real good doctors with some good medicine and people are living a lot longer." She winked and smiled, the wrinkles in her face reminded me of an old road map that exposed many travels in her time. Her eyes were tired and she was tired. I reached over and grabbed her hand and smiled back at her. I told her I would try to tell people about her bad dream in the only way I knew. I walked over to the computer and started clicking away........

Garbage dumpsite　　Scavengers
environment　　Man and resources
crude　　　greed
multi-colored lakes of oil　　Skin ripped off flesh
slickly for power　　luxurious fur coats
threat of war
treehuggers, oh those darn heathens
watersheds filled in between large uranium deposits
economic environment disasters
ACT III : A DEAD EARTH filled
with death spirits

the voices echoed through the ozone while
crystal waters screamed in pain
roots of trees clogged with smelters welting the hillside
Her flesh and bones rotted amongst piles of nuclear waste
I kept wondering if we call the police before the rape or after?
911 I have an emergency.... yes it's the earth we are in trouble ...please
send someone right way we can't afford to lose this one......

Operator: "We'll decide that.... can I put you on hold? Thank you."

** CLICK **

Ice Screams

It's been three days and I am still here, sitting in this back corner, away from everyone. Three days.

People look at me funny. Most of them had been there the first night I'd come in and were surprised to still see me sitting in the corner when they came back but I didn't care. I would just order another drink, but that's why they look at me funny. I wasn't known as a particularly hard drinker; in fact only a handful of people in this bar could claim to have ever seen me drunk once, let along for three straight days.

I knew they are all dying to ask me what happened out there on the ice but that would defeat the purpose of drinking. I'd have to remember

So instead I sat here, listening to the same country songs played on the jukebox over and over again. If it had been a weekend, there would have been a hand, but not in the middle of the week. The waitress kept eyeing me warily. I guess years of training taught her to watch people who power drink. But I was no problem. I just wanted to be left alone, drink some more rye and try to burn some memory cells.

Stan and David came in earlier and tried to join me but I made it obvious I was not fit for company. I kinda got the feeling my mother probably sent them to talk sense into me or at least keep an eye on me. But Mom knew what happened, and she knew I had to work this out myself. Though I doubt she agreed with my methods; as everyone knows, fear and alcohol often hold hands.

The "Drinking Don't Kill Me, Her Memory Will" song started to play. What little feeling I had left was tempted to smile at the irony. Except in this case, it would be this memory and it sure as hell wasn't a love story.

It had been three days since Ryan's incident but the thought of what happened still scared the hell out of me, a good four bottles of rye later. The sharp reports from the pool table make me think of my buddy William. Normally he'd be at that table exercising one of the few talents he has in life. I wondered what he's doing now, probably hiding at home, since he doesn't drink any more.

Stan and David get up to leave. They've been there a good three hours, keeping an eye on me. They've done their good deed but they have families and work tomorrow. They look at me, then open the door to leave. A cold blast poured in and in the distance I can see the multicolored light of this small town stretching down the street. Stan and David see the numbed look on my face, shudder and then leave.

They will probably take the 507 to the cut-off, then drive across the lake to the village. People have short memories when they are in a hurry. The lake usually freezes over by this time of year, taking a good sixteen minutes off the trip into town. People from the village always travelled across the lake, even before most people had cars. Years ago people drove sleighs or even walked across the two mile lake. It was usually safe from mid-December to early March, supposedly.

Having grown up there all their lives, most of the local people can handle the frozen lake. That's what makes what happened to Ryan's parents so puzzling. What happened shouldn't have happened. It was late February, a safe enough month. All the winter sales were beginning and his parents, always frugal shoppers, decided to go all the way to Toronto to spend four days shopping. It was all planned. Being only 9 at the time, Ryan got to go with them while his older sister stayed behind with relatives.

I was told that Ryan was always particularly close to his parents,closer then his older sister. My mother claimed it was because he was a difficult birth. Story had it his mother almost died giving birth to him and then he almost died of some respiratory problem a week later. His mother blamed the nursing staff, saying they didn't watch over him enough. Then his father accused this one nurse of being racist and prejudiced against Indians. You had to know Ryan's parents.

Needless to say, they both survived. Maureen, his mother, liked to say she refused to even consider dying until she knew if her little one would be okay. That sort of set the pattern for the rest of their lives.

By pattern I meant he was the baby of the family and was treated like that. It was a little obvious that he was favoured by the parents but that happened in some families. Of course that was not to say the parents neglected or didn't love Aricka, his sister. He just got the benefit of the doubt, or the bigger slice of the pie. Pretty soon Aricka learned to accept that, though it was through gritted teeth. It's amazing Ryan didn't grow up more spoiled then he really was.

I remembered how excited Ryan was about going to Toronto. He'd never been there before. Aricka, fours years older, shrugged off his enthusiasm, a little hurt she wasn't going. All she had to look forward to was a week of exams and staying with her aunt.

Standing at the school bus stop that fateful morning, all she talked about was her brother and the trip. Minus 10 degrees and she could still whine.

"He always gets what he wants. Mom treats him better then me. She always does. He's the baby," she says. "If you baby someone all the time then they'll be a baby all the time."

I stamped my poor frozen 13 year old feet in response. The school bus was late, probably due to the heavy falling snow. A possible day off from school was rolling around in all our minds so we didn't care much about Ryan or Aricka's problem.

All except for William. William Williams was my best friend then and now, and don't ask me why. It just was. He could be an idiot sometimes, most times, but I accepted that. It was one of those friendships that defied explanation. Now William had little affection for Ryan either. Ryan had never done anything against William or vice versa so there was no real grounds for his dislike. You had to keep in mind William's reasoning was that of a thirteen-year old. He hated the attention Ryan got from his parents because William was somewhere in the middle in a family of nine. You had to fight hard for any recognition at his house. But I suspected the real reason came from a secret crush he had on Aricka. He would agree with anything she said just to get on her good side.

"It must be terrible having a brother like that," he said sympathetically. He could always be counted on to be sympathetic to a pretty girl when it was necessary, even at that age and temperature.

Aricka watched the family truck approach through the growing snowfall. You got used to it. Someday though, he wouldn't always be the favourite. He wouldn't be so hot then. The little scum.

Then the family Ford came rolling down the street, on its way toToronto. The family was ready to buy out the town and fit as much of it as they could into their beat-up old vehicle. It was a yearly thing with that family and a few others on the Reserve: the income tax refund came in early and already it was mentally spent.

The last anybody saw of them was the beat-up end of their truck roaring down towards the lake, a trail of snow and exhaust billowing up through the snow flakes.

I remembered Ryan sticking his tongue out at Aricka as they disappeared into the whiteness of the lake.

Aricka blew into her hands. "I hope they get a flat," she said. William responded with a hearty "Yeah" and smiled like someone who's just scored some victory points.

After that it got kind of strange. Three days passed before Mags Magneen noticed a light on at Ryan's house as she was driving by. According to what she knew, they were still supposed to be in Toronto. No car was in the driveway and nobody answered the phone. Always the curious (and some would say nosey) type, she decided to investigate.

The way she told it the house looked as cold as a Christian's heart as she surveyed it. A blanket of virgin snow seemed to surround the house. She had to break a trail as she walked up to the front door. The light was still on but the house felt empty, as she put it.

A couple of knocks on the door went unanswered, as did the harder pounding that followed. Feeling somewhat uneasy, Mags was going to give up and leave but decided to give it one last try and rattled the door knob. She discovered the door was unlocked. Puzzled, she swung it open

"Martin? Audrey? Are you here? Hello." No answer again. She shivered, not sure if it was from the cold or the eerie silence. The house was cold, colder then outside it seemed. Some of the lights were on but the place still looked dark. Mags called out a few times but other than the unnerving echo of an empty house, there was no response. The kitchen was clean as always and Mags was confused. It wasn't like Ryan's family to leave the lights on when they went away, let alone leaving the door unlocked. Yet, they weren't there and weren't due back for a few days.

She wandered into the living room and looked around. Again, nothing looked like it had been touched in a few days, except for the comforter on their big couch. Mags had given it to Ryan's mother four years before. Now it was lying all in a bundle alone corner of the couch.

Mags was beginning to feel the February cold by this time and was tempted to leave, maybe make a few phone calls later to some relatives inquiring about the location of the family. Still puzzled over the strange situation of the house, she absentmindedly picked up the comforter from the couch and started to fold it.

Ryan looked back at her from under the comforter. Mags screamed and jumped a good six feet back, across the worn out Lazyboy and then up against the window, knocking over a plant. Ryan, his expression never changing, followed her with his brown eyes.

"My God, Ryan, you scared the hell out of me! What are you doing underneath that blanket?"

Ryan merely looked at her, still not saying anything.

"Ryan, are you okay? Where are your parents?"

Ryan shivered, picked up the rapidly discarded comforter, and pulled it back over him. He disappeared back into the couch as quickly as he had appeared.

"Ryan?" Mags tried again. Again no answer. She approached the couch again, more timidly this time, still calling out Ryan's name, with the same lack of response as before. Her gloved hand reached out slowly and tugged at the comforter until Ryan's face and upper body were visible.

"Ryan, what happened to you?" Ryan merely blinked his eyes at her and shivered again.

According to Mags, poor Ryan looked like hell. He was still in the same clothes he had worn when he and the family had driven off the Reserve 3 days ago. His face held no expression, just a steady blankness, and it was thinner. The doctor later estimated that 9 year-old Ryan had lost 6 lbs in 3 days.

A nervous Mags covered Ryan in the comforter and another blanket from the overturned lazyboy. Ryan didn't flinch, didn't move. You could barely see the little trickle of vapour escaping from his mouth into the cold air. Mags then searched every room but couldn't find anything that would explain Ryan's mysterious presence.

The kitchen was untouched, some of the plants were dead from the cold. It was in the kitchen where Mags found the reason for the intense cold. A large window overlooking the back yard had been forced open and left that way. Footprints outside the window led away into the bushes, towards the lake. They were the same size as Ryan's feet. Mags was beginning to get real scared.

"Ryan, listen to me. Where are your parents? Did they leave you here?" Ryan didn't respond; instead, he tried to duck under the comforter again. Mags quickly grabbed his arm and immediately let go again. "Your arms are so cold."

Ryan stopped moving for a moment, looked at Mags, his brown eyes both looking and not looking into hers.

"Cold," was all he said.

That was enough for Mags. The police were there in 15 minutes. Aricka was driven in from school; uncles, aunts, and cousins all converged on that little house. But still Ryan refused to talk. The more they asked questions, the more blank he got. Aricka was getting panicky; at one point she screamed at Ryan to ask where their parents were. She had to be dragged out of the room and looked after by the doctor. The doctor then quickly examined Ryan, but it was obvious what was wrong. Hungry, dehydrated, suffering from hyperthermia, and, of course, shock.

One of the cops followed the footprints as far as he could. He got as far as the lake but by then the wind had obliterated any trace of a trail. They later theorized that Ryan had been in the house for the last three days, not eating or doing anything, just sitting there under the comforter and occasionally going to the bathroom. That became fruitless after the pipes froze and burst the first night.

"Where are his parents?" became the question for the cops. Everybody had a good idea as to the answer but they were afraid to voice it.

It was Mags who took the first step. After some prodding, her husband finally agreed to take two of the Constables out on the lake to follow the winter road across the lake.

They were out a little over a mile, travelling slowly and studying the surface intently, when they came across a break in the shallow snow wall that lines the winter road. It was almost invisible, hidden by the three day old fallen snow. After that it wasn't long before they found the remains of a trail. A trail that ended abruptly at some freshly frozen ice.

The police later theorized that Ryan's parents got lost in the thick snowstorm that was falling that morning and veered off the main road towards the channel. A half mile later, they went through the ice. Somehow, Ryan must have gotten out of the car and crawled onto the safe ice. He liked riding with the back window open because sometimes he got car sick. He must have walked home, soaking wet, through the snowstorm and sub-zeroweather, and then broke into his own home.

And three days later he was found. They never found the car though because the lake was over two hundred feet deep.

Even to this day, a good quarter of the village won't drive across the lake because of what happened. People said it was just an accident but you could still see the shudder sweep across the people when they talked about it, usually around freeze-up or melt-down.

Oh sure, every winter some fool people went through the ice like clockwork. It was usually some white cottagers who decided to go out to try their new snowmobiles on the lake too early or too late in the season. Or sometimes they raced across the lake, forgot where they were going, and drifted a little too close to the channel where the ice was thinner because of the current.

Most of the Native people didn't go ice-fishing near the channel after Kid Johnson caught what he thought was a hell of a big fish there one spring. The Kid, as we called him, still won't eat fish to this day.

Eventually they took Ryan to the hospital. They considered taking Aricka too but one of the aunts convinced the doctor she could take care of her better. The cops wandered around aimlessly, ill at ease and confused. There were no bad guys to chase, no bodies to identify or take away, no tickets to write.

All they had were two kids, one pretty well catatonic, and a big hole in the lake. Pretty soon they packed up and left the house to the relatives.

I remembered playing in the snow as the cop cars drove by our house. Us kids hadn't heard the news yet but my parents had. They looked sombrely out the window at the retreating cars. We knew something was up, but when you had two feet of good snow to play in, who cared?

But that night, everybody knew, regardless of age. Contrary to popular belief, not a lot of exciting things happened on reserves.The news was to keep the phone lines tied up for at least a good month.

Once the news got around, a bunch of us kids would gather by the shore of the channel and look out towards the section of lake where the car went in, looking vainly for anything out of the ordinary. Like we were expecting the car to come driving out through the ice, or at the very least Audrey and Martin's ghost suddenly appearing to a half-dozen partially-frozen children.

Aricka was back in school within three days. Some of her closest friends surrounded her and offered companionship and support kidstyle. But the majority of us wouldn't go near her if we could help it. If we bumped into her in the hall we'd say hello and all that, but that was the extent of it. For some reason she seemed tainted with something dark and we didn't want to have anything to do with it. And William swore off his crush on her, preferring fresh game. I even felt guilty about avoiding her.

But one place I couldn't avoid her was in class. I sat beside her in history. Usually a talkative girl, all day she'd just stare at her books, occasionally looking up when the teacher spoke. The teachers knew enough not to call on her for any questions, which surprised most of us who always doubted the common sense of most teachers.

At one point her pencil broke, and she fumbled around in her pencil case for another. She always liked writing in pencil,saying it gave her a chance to rethink things. I offered her mine-I'm a pen-type guy. She looked at me. I think I even caught a bit of a smile from her.

"Thanks." She took it and went back to work. That was our conversation for the day.

Ryan on the other hand was a different story. He was in the hospital for two weeks, in bad shape. His body temperature was really low and other problems were happening. He wouldn't eat, wouldn't do nothing. They even brought in one of them psychiatrists but with little results. It was like talking to adisconnected telephone.

One day, about a week after my conversation with Aricka, me and William paid him a visit. Actually that wasn't quite correct. Rather, my mother, in exchange for a trip into town to see a movie, told William and me we'd be making a pit stop at the hospital, whether we wanted to or not. It was sort of Mom's Reserve version of home psychiatric treatment. Only dogs could talk to dogs and only kids can talk to kids.

William was not amused. The last thing he wanted was to spend a Saturday afternoon in a hospital talking to some orphan kid gone crazy that he never liked in the first place. William was like that.

And to tell the truth, I didn't want to be there much myself, but neither of us could or would say "no" to my mother.

"I hate your mother," was all William could say as we walked down the antiseptic-smelling snow-white hallway.

That's how we found ourselves going into room 413, an ominous number if ever we'd heard one.

The door was open and we entered. We could see him from where we stood. Ryan was almost lost in the sheets. We were surprised at how different he looked, how much weight he'd lost. He almost disappeared into the pillow and sheets; only his dark skin told us where he was.

We shuffled nervously, neither of us wanting to break the silence in the room. There were two other beds in the room; one was empty and the other had some white kid reading a stack of comic books. Ryan seemed oblivious to everything.

Finally I broke the silence. "Hey Ryan, how you doing?" The silence returned. William and I looked at each other.

"He doesn't talk. He's kinda spooky." It was the comic book kid, some redhead with a leg in a cast.

"He hasn't said anything at all?"

"Nope. The nurses, the doctors, everybody talks to him but he doesn't say anything. Why's he in here anyways?"

A little more reassured that Ryan wouldn't jump up and grab him, William edged a little closer to Ryan, his curiosity getting the best of him.

"His parents went through the ice in a car," I said.

The comic book kid looked surprised. "They put you in the hospital for that?"

"He was in the back seat. Barely got out. I think that's why he's like this," I found myself edging closer. By now we were both at the bedside, looking at Ryan. Seeing all the tubes and medical stuff running everywhere almost made the trip worthwhile.

"Ryan?" No response. "It's Andrew and William."

William managed a feeble "Hi." Ryan couldn't manage even that.

"I told you." The comic book kid was getting annoying. William looked at me.

"Well, we tried. Let's go. The movie starts in half an hour." William was already edging his body towards the door but for some weird, no doubt morbid reason, I was fascinated by Ryan. I didn't want to leave just yet.

"Look at his face. I wonder what he's thinking about? What do you think, William?"

"I don't know. The Flintstones. Let's go."

"He looks cold."

"Not any more." This time the voice came from Ryan. If it were possible for two 13-year-olds to have heart attacks, that was the time. Even the comic book kid looked up in surprise.

"Ryan?" My voice quivered. Slowly he turned to look at me. The glazed lack of expression had left his face. He now looked like he was either concentrating or constipated.

"I'm in a hospital?" William and I could only nod. "My parents are dead, aren't they?"

Again we nodded.

"I'm hungry."

William, still a bit nervous, reached in his pocket and brought out a package of gum. He removed one stick and held out his hand towards Ryan. "It's all I got."

Ryan looked at it for a moment, then reached over and grabbed it. The moment his hand touched the gum William jerked his hand away.

"Thanks." Ryan then mechanically removed the wrapper and put it in his mouth. The chewing looked like it took some effort. The only noise that could be heard in the room was the sound of gum chewing and comic book pages being turned.

After some moments of silence, Ryan pulled himself up in bed and looked out the window. "So, what's new?" he asked.

"Ryan, are you okay?" I always seemed to find myself in the role of the perpetual big brother. Ryan still was not looking at us; he stared into the glaring sunlight.

"Yeah, I guess."

"How come you haven't talked in a week?"

"I don't know. I just kept seeing Mom and Dad in the car, going through the ice. And pretty soon, I didn't want to see that any more, so I went to sleep."

"But you were awake."

"Didn't feel like it. Then I heard your voices, like in school, and I remembered I have a test in Math. Mom always liked me doing good in Math. How about that, my mom was right. Only dogs can talk to dogs."

"Um. That was four days ago."

"Guess I failed, huh?" Then his whole body started to shake. His face contorted and it was obvious what was coming next. The sobs rolled out of him, gradually becoming louder and louder till they filled the room. They were gut-wrenching and it looked almost painful. Everybody had seen crying before but this wasn't ordinary. We bolted for the door, grabbed the first nurse we saw and pointed her in Ryan's direction. Then we got the hell out of there. We'd seen enough scary things for the day. Needless to say, we didn't enjoy the movie much.

The next day at school Aricka made a beeline for me on my way in. "I heard you visited my brother yesterday."

After what had happened, crying and all, I wasn't sure if this was necessarily a good thing or not. So I tried to play it cool. "Yeah. We dropped by."

"Thanks. He's talking now."

I shuffled my feet. "And crying."

"Yeah but the doctors say that's good. What did you say to him?"

"Nothing really. Just said hello and talked about how cold he looked. That's all."

Aricka smiled at me. "Well, what ever you did, thank you." Then she leaned over and did the most amazing thing. She kissed me on the cheek. I'd never been kissed on the cheek before, I'd never been kissed anywhere. It was the strangest feeling I'd ever had; my insides were melting and I would have died for this 13 year old girl but I was terrified that someone would have seen us. I figured I was too young to die of embarrassment. I just stood there, stunned. And she was still standing there too. "Could you do me another favour?"

Barely trusting myself to talk, I managed to sputter out "What?"

"Help me do something. Come with me out on the lake."

I came to instantly. "Are you crazy? Your parents just.... well you know."

"I want to put some flowers on the spot where they....were. I was so mad at them when they left, I'll feel better if I say goodbye. Please come with me."

There was no way I was going to go out on that ice ever in my lifetime, let alone within 10 days of what happened. Not for any girl.

"Sure. When?"

She smiled the most incredible smile. "Tomorrow, after school." She kissed me again and went in the school. That set the future pattern for the many stupid things I would find myself doing for women over the next dozen years.

The next thirty hours were less than enjoyable. The thought of going out onto that ice terrified me. The weather was getting warmer yet my feet were getting colder. All through school the next day she would smile and give me the thumbs up. Finally 3 o'clock rolled around, as did my stomach.

She was to meet me at the doors of the school. I was half tempted to make a run for it but I had made a promise. I was scared but proud.

The last few students made their way through the doors; then she showed up.

She solemnly buttoned up her coat. "Let's go. We have to stop at my house first," she said.

It was there where she picked up her flowers. She had moved back into the house about a week ago and one of her unmarried aunts had moved in with her. Somehow she had scammed her aunt into getting some flowers for her, saying they were going to the grave site.

"I'll deal with my aunt later," she said as she gathered the flowers up. This was the first time I'd been in that house since it happened. It was unnerving. Nothing looked changed, except an 8 x 10 picture of the family that had once been a 5 x 7. The smiling eyes of Audrey and Martin seem to stare out at me. So did Ryan's.

We retraced the same steps Ryan had used from the lake to the house. There was already a path broken in the snow: Aricka was talking on about the state of her family but I couldn't listen. I kept thinking about Ryan walking the entire distance, wet, and a zombie. I shivered from more then the cold. Aricka led the way, her arms full of roses. I followed.

"Ryan's doing good. Doctors say he can come home in a few days. I saw him last night. He misses me, and the family, but he won't talk about Mom and Pop. The doctors say not to force him."

I almost tripped over a buried log and stumbled off the path. In the freshly overturned snow, I saw a flash of red. I picked it up and it was a red mitten of some sort.

"Aricka? What colour were Ryan's mitts?"

Aricka trudged on, without even looking back. "Red. Why?"

I threw it away like it was covered in ants. "No reason."

We finally made the windswept lake. I tried to see the other side but the glare from the snow made me squint. Walking on the ice was a lot easier. The constant wind had packed the snow quite well, giving it a little padding, almost like walking on long grass.

The wind howled by us as I stupidly put one foot in front of the other, wishing I was anywhere but here. Aricka led the way, a good two feet in front of me. I couldn't help but think that if my family knew I was out here, I might as well go through the ice. I tried to look through the blinding glare to make sure nobody could see us, or even just identify me.

Suddenly Aricka stopped, then I stopped. We had been walking for about twenty minutes until we came to a place where it was obvious a lot of people had been standing around. Cigarette butts littered the area, as well as the odd pee stain. The police had been here. And there, in the centre of everything, was a refrozen jagged blot in the lake. I couldn't take my eyes off of it, knowing that somewhere beneath it, a couple of hundred feet or so, was a 1970 Ford with two overweight Indians in it. And they would probably be there forever.

Aricka stood there for a moment. Then she took a deep breath and walked forward. Her foot gingerly tested the new ice but by then it had frozen solid enough to support the weight of a 13 year-old girl. She walked to the centre of the blot, and kneeled. She put the roses down gently and seemed to pet them for a moment. Freezing, but not wanting to say anything, I shuffled from one foot to another.

"Good bye, Mom, Pop. I'll remember you." I think she was crying but I couldn't see because of her coat hood. In the coldness of the lake, I was worried the tears might freeze.

We remained like that for a few minutes before she stood up and started walking back to the shore. Thanking God with every step, I followed.

Without looking at me, she had to shout above the blowing of the wind. "It's over now. Thanks, Andrew."

Even out on that frigid lake, I felt a little warmer.

Then she stopped and turned around. She had been crying. "I know you didn't want to come but you did. I knew nobody else would come with me. Or they'd try and talk me out of it. Thanks so much."

Then surprise number two happened. She grabbed me and hugged me. A little embarrassed but instinctively my hands went around her. She wasn't crying or anything, it just felt like she wanted to hold on to something. Out on that barren lake, I guess I was the only thing.

After that, we quietly went home.

Ryan came home a few days later, looking more sombre then ever. They had managed to put some weight on him but he still looked small. Hoping for another hug and kiss I went over to visit them. Ryan almost looked normal, but there was still something about him, something that hovered about him crying out that this kid has seen some seriously scary stuff.

He still wouldn't talk about his parents, or what really happened that day. All the doctors were worried about that but Ryan didn't care. Neither did Aricka. She was just happy to have him back. And to think just two weeks ago, she had called him a little scum.

By the summer Ryan had pretty well become his old self. He was playing with his old friends again, doing things, even laughing. There was a big party on his tenth birthday. I was there, and I even managed to bring William. It was held down at his aunt's place near the tip of the lake. After all the festivities had happened, everybody decided to go swimming. The lake was alive with the sound of splashing and laughing kids.

All except for Ryan. He refused to go in the water. He just sat on the dock watching, occasionally waving. But he never went in the water that day. He blamed it on a cold he had but there was something more. The fact that he never went swimming, canoeing, fishing, anything water-related ever again in his life, let me believe I was on to something. Aricka just shrugged it off.

"He'll get over it. Don't worry."

Aricka and I were spending a lot of time together. By the first anniversary of the accident, we were officially an item. Again she talked me into accompanying her out onto the ice, and again we put the roses down, though we had trouble finding the exact spot. We hung out together until we were 17, and then the time came for me to go off to college. It was an amiable separation, we just grew apart.

She got a new boyfriend and every time that anniversary rolled around, she'd drag that poor sucker out onto the ice with her. Same with the one after him. But eventually she married a guy from the reserve a couple years ago and moved to Peterborough, about a half hour from home.

Ryan did well at school, even became a decent baseball player, but he never left the Reserve for any length of time. He never had the inclination to go anywhere or do anything. He still lives in his parents house and I'd see them occasionally when I came home. I even went out drinking with Ryan a few times. And whenever I wasn't around, William would keep me informed as to what was happening around the village. William was quite happy. He ran the local marina and living with a beautiful girl named Angela. He had everything he wanted, except a charge account at the beer store.

Me? I kicked around the city a bit, doing a little of this, a little of that. I came home every couple of months, though, to recharge my batteries. I finally came home two years ago at the ripe old age of 24. Now I had a steady girlfriend, and an occasional job at the band office, whenever they threw me a contract like somebody throws a dog a bone.

But in my two years back home, I realized more then ever how true that old saying was. 'The more things change, the more they stay the same.' The village had a few more houses, a little less forest. In some of the local bars, I ran into cousins I used to babysit. These little things didn't add up to much when you considered that the tone of the village was the same. To this day, most people didn't know what was going on up at the band office, and didn't really care. Old people still sat by their window looking out at the cars driving by, dogs running everywhere fertilizing the world. Home was home, what could you say?

It was winter again and I was back staying at my mother's when Aricka called. It was the first time I'd spoken with her in almost a year or so. Teenage romances are hardly binding ten years later. Especially when you live in two different towns.

"Andrew? I hate calling you like this out of the blue but I need your help."

She still had that breathless quality about the way she talked. When we were young I think it came from girlish enthusiasm, her brain working faster then her mouth, but now I feared it was from too many cigarettes.

"You sound serious, what's up?"

"It's anniversary time."

I knew it was this week. You didn't forget a thing like that but I had long ago stopped being a part of her ritual.

"Yeah, I remember. I hear you still go out on the ice with them flowers of yours."

"Not this year. I'm pregnant, Andrew. The doctor says I could deliver anytime. He and Richard won't allow me to go out on the ice this year."

I almost dropped the phone in surprise. "Don't tell me you want me to go out there!"

She was quick to respond. "Now calm down, Andrew. Richard offered to but Ryan told him no. He wants to do it."

"But he never goes out on the lake, summer or winter."

"Well, he is this year. I don't feel right about it. It scares me. You know he's never been right about water since the accident. Something could happen out there."

I knew where this was leading. "Yeah, so?"

There was a deep breath on the other end. "Go with him, Andrew. Make sure everything's all right."

"Why me? You've got more cousins and relatives then you know what to do with. I don't want to sound rude but why me?"

"I was thinking about that too," her voice got softer. "You brought Ryan out of what ever he was in, remember, in the hospital? And you went out with me that first time. I knew you didn't want to go but you did. It has to be you, Andrew. Promise me you will?"

I was silent for a moment. Those feelings from thirteen years ago came back to the pit of my stomach. I was cornered. "You win. I'll go."

Aricka was ecstatic. She thanked me profusely but I barely heard her.

I was thinking about how to handle this. I'd found that as you get older, your sense of courage tended to evaporate, disappear like the wind that blows across frozen lakes. I had promised I would go, but I wouldn't go alone. I immediately phoned up my buddy, my pal William.

He was not pleased, even less than me. "I don't even like the guy. It's your promise, you deal with it."

Luckily the gods had allowed me to go to a hockey tournament a few months back with William. There we met these two girls from another Reserve and, well, so on. Also as the gods would allow, I had Angela's phone number, his long-suffering girlfriend. I casually mentioned this to William. You have to do these things with William, just to keep him in line. That's what friends are for.

He was flustered for a moment. "I'll tell Barb," he said. "Then you'll be in trouble." I could hear the smile growing in his voice.

I wasn't going out with Barb at the time. "See you tomorrow at five. Bye." Before he could protest, I hung up.

I picked him up in my car the following day. He was glum, cranky and generally not impressed with me. "I hope you're happy," he said. I was, sort of, as happy as I could be, under the conditions. "Let's just get this over with." Good old William, the milk of humanity overflowed in him.

We arrived at Ryan's house, and it had changed little since that winter thirteen years before. Maybe a little more run down (bachelors are like that), but not much. Ryan was already sitting on the porch, his hair blowing in the stiff wind. A bouquet of half-frozen flowers on the porch beside him. You could tell he didn't want to do this, even from this distance but he had to.

Something inside was going to make him do it. It was necessary. Like going to the dentist.

"I really don't want to do this, Andrew," said William.

"Neither do I, but we gotta."

"My, aren't we plural these days?"

Once our car stopped in his driveway, he got up and walked over, breath pouring out of his mouth like a little steam engine. I opened my window to talk to him.

"Hey Ryan, ready to go?"

Instead, he opened my door and motioned for me and William to get out.

"Let's cut through the woods. It will be quicker than driving around to the lake, then walking. It's about half the distance."

William looked at me with worry. We would be following the same path Ryan took coming back from the accident, and we were going to the lake to remember the accident. This was becoming too much for William, almost too much for me. Ryan motioned for us to get out of the vehicle again and we did. I could hear William muttering under his breath, "You owe me big, Andrew."

"Well, let's go."

Ryan closed the door behind me and started walking across his yard towards the woods a hundred feet distant. He quickly grabbed the flowers and nestled them in his arms. William and I followed along like ducklings behind their mother, every once in a while William giving me a shove to remind me he was here at my insistence, or actually, threat. Nobody said anything until we reached the lake.

I'd never been one for ice fishing. I always found it too cold, and the fish was never tasty enough to warrant the cold. Still, I always found myself out on the lake for one reason or another at least once a year, the same with William. But this was the first time for Ryan in all these years, winter or summer. He stopped walking just short of the ice. He looked out across the frozen expanse. I couldn't tell if he was working up nerve or lost in thought.

"It's been so long, I wasn't sure where it was." His voice was almost lost in the rushing wind. "Aricka sort of gave me directions. A little off to the right of the spit, she said." We all mentally found the spit, then the direction. "That way, I guess."

Nobody moved. Again William was muttering to himself, "Oh Angela, where are you? Your arms are so warm? February on our Reserve can make you very romantic." Then suddenly Ryan was out on the ice, walking at a brisk pace. We were a good ten feet behind him before we started moving to catch up.

Other than the wind, the only thing we could hear was the dry crunching of lake snow under our three sets of boots. Again we walked in a row, barely able to keep up with Ryan. There were old skidoo tracks all around us. It would have made walking a lot easier by following them but Ryan had his own course set.

Approximately half way to our destination William finally said something aloud. "For God's sakes, Ryan, slow down. My sweat is freezing."

Ryan stopped and looked around. "Oh sorry, I wasn't thinking. Actually, I was thinking too much."

"What's the hurry?" William looked miserable, his hands shoved way down deep in his pockets.

Ryan started to walk again. "No hurry, just lost in thought. It's all so familiar. Except it's not snowing."

Again William muttered to himself, "Give it time."

We were walking again but not so fast. The shoreline was slowly drifting off behind us, and we were squinting now from the glare.

William tightened his hood to keep the wind out. "Been a while,huh, Ryan?"

Ryan looked like he wasn't listening but he was.

"Yeah, a while." He kept walking. "You two didn't have to come with me, you know. I could have handled it myself."

"I know but your sister asked me as a favour. You know I could never say no to Aricka." This was true even now, pregnant and all.

"I almost wish you hadn't come, Andrew. You make it more real. I remember the two of you at the hospital, then the crying. It's like I'm 9 years old again."

The wind started to pick up and we soon found ourselves shouting three feet from each other. In another few minutes we'd be there.

"You know, I always told people I really couldn't remember what went on that day, when they died. Actually I do but I never wanted to talk about it. At the time I thought it was nobody's business, not even Aricka's. She wasn't there, she didn't see anything. Now I don't know."

We were approaching the channel; a couple hundred feet to the left was the other shore. The ice would still be quite safe but it was like looking over the edge of a tall building, you knew you were safe but...

"I was sitting in the back, the window was open. You remember how I used to get car sick? Dad was cursing about the snow, worried that he might be lost. Mom had just told me to roll it up, it was too cold to have it open. That's when it happened."

"The car just lurched, dropped and I was thrown to the floor. Mom was screaming and I heard Dad call my name. Then I felt wet, and very cold. I climbed on the back seat, and saw water coming in my open window.

I don't know if it was instinct or what but I jumped through that window so fast its all a blur."

William and I felt like we were being told a ghost story, in a very ghostly place, with a very ghostly person. It wasn't a very warm feeling. I was beginning to wish Angela was here too.

"I was only little then," Ryan continued speaking. "So the ice could hold me up. I crawled across the broken ice to the solid stuff. It was cold, so damn cold, but it soon went away. I actually felt numb, then warm after awhile. All the time I could hear Mom and Dad behind me. They were trying to open their doors, but because of the water pressure, the doors wouldn't open."

"You don't have to tell us this." William said what I was thinking.

I don't think Ryan heard, either because of the wind, or the memory.

"I remember sitting on the ice, crying. The water was up to the windows, and there were bubbles everywhere. It looked like it was boiling. Mom rolled down her window and tried to crawl through but she was kinda big. She wouldn't fit, I've never seen her try so hard at anything. She actually looked wedged in the window, then she reached for me, like she wanted me to pull her out, or maybe pull me in with her. I don't know. But the look on her face... It was then the car went under the water, with a large plopping sound. It wasn't there any more. There were more bubbles then her purse floated to the surface."

Ryan stopped both talking and walking. Evidently we had reached the spot, or as close to it as we were going to find, both in his memory and our reality. He was looking down at the ice about six feet ahead of him.

"I just sat there for the longest time. I was nine years old, I didn't really know what was going on. I was scared, cold, in shock. After that it gets kind of blurry. I guess I found my way home."

Way over on the other side of the lake, I could see a car driving across the ice, heading to the reserve. I wished I was in it.

"Is this why you've never been out on the lake since?"

"I guess. I just remember my Mom reaching for me. They're still out here, you know. Somewhere below us. They never found the bodies."

William stamped his feet from both impatience and cold. "Can we get on with this please?"

"You're right. Let's get this over with." Ryan walked ahead a bit, then kneeled down and placed the flowers quietly on the ice. Then he started to stroke the flowers, like he was afraid to leave them. "Since the accident, I've always been afraid of this place. But Jesus, I'm twenty-two years old! You've got to stop being afraid at some point. In all this time I've never been able to say goodbye to them. After all, its only water, right?" "Good bye Dad. Good bye Mom." He stood up and turned to face us, a slight smile on his face. "I was always Mom's favourite."

It was then he went through the ice. It all happened so quickly. There was a sharp cracking noise, Ryan looked down, and then, like bread in a toaster, he slid straight down into the water, the ice buckling around the edge of the hole. A plume of water rushed up to take his place for a scant few seconds before falling onto the ice.

Then there was silence, even the sound of our breathing had stopped. We stood there for a moment, not believing what we've just seen. I remember instinctively racing for the hole and William grabbing me and wrestling me to the ground. I tried to crawl to the hole but he held me.

"Forget it man, he's gone. He's under the ice somewhere. We'll never find him."

William was right, there was no sign of Ryan in the three-foot hole, just the occasional bubble.

"Come on, man. Lets just get the hell out of here. Tell the police."

We stood up. I looked at the hole again, not knowing what to do. "Don't, Andrew, let's go." William grabbed my arm and turned me towards home. We slowly headed back to the shore.

William took one last look backwards. "Like he said, he always was his mother's favourite."

On the way back, it started to snow.

That was three days ago. Three long days ago. We told the police; they went out with divers but never found anything. I never thought they would. The community went into mourning, and the funeral was today. Even drunk I found it mildly amusing - them burying a body they never found.

Poor William. Fortunately or unfortunately, depending on how you look at it, he doesn't drink. From what I've heard he hasn't come out of his house in the last few days, won't take calls either. The police had to practically threaten to arrest him if he didn't give them a statement.

And here I sit, waiting for the waitress to walk by so I can order another drink. I keep seeing Ryan disappearing into the ice over and over and over again. I now have a new respect for alcoholics and why they drink. While I don't think this phase will last forever (I'm really a terrible alcoholic), it will hopefully last till I have new thoughts to think, and new memories.

I have just enough time to make last call. I manage to flag down the waitress as she passes. She nods at me.

"Yeah, yeah, I know. Double Rye and coke, no ice."

The End.

William Oanasan

Death and Life at the Round Valley Reservation

1

across the salty distance
and decades of grief since Hiroshima
shadows of holocaust fall over
the valley and earth
2

turn the clouds of fire and carnage
toward yellow poppies, blackberries and acorns
the way leaves of cherry trees and rice stalks
turn sunlight in Hiroshima

Sheila Sanderson

Power: Who Really Pays the Cost?

Since the dawn of capitalism, industrialized societies have expanded at unprecedented rates. One fundamental factor which has enabled this rapid expansion has been the ability to fulfill increasing energy demands. John Bodley (author of Anthropology and Contemporary Human Problems) has warned that "Resources are being consumed at a rate greater than they are being produced by natural, biological or geological processes..." (1985:38). He has determined that this effect is not strictly due to an increase in population, but rather the result of a problem of over-consumption in industrialized societies (1985:39).

Within the context of Canadian society, the relationships between overpopulation and over-consumption are easily illustrated, particularly with regard to urban centers and industry. The denser populations of Canada's southern regions tend to over-consume and thus require more and more energy to sustain themselves as time progresses. Industry promotes the consumption of goods which they produce by making them appear desirable, and even necessary. The production of many of these goods requires a significant amount of energy. As the population density of cities rises, industry grows and demands for energy increase. However, as the film The Limits of Growth has indicated, the expansion of industry and its energy requirements cannot continue very much longer without risking a total collapse of the systems which sustain us.

In an effort to meet new and growing demands for energy, Canada's federal and provincial governments have sought out new sources of energy which are relatively inexpensive to tap and which are regarded as sustainable. The hydroelectric potential of Canada's many large river systems is enormous.

Waldram has noted that while "small scale water power projects have (historically) been common throughout the country....it is only in the last few decades that engineering developments have produced a dramatic change in the focus of hydro development" (1988:7). This focus has shifted to megaprojects which, although capable of harnessing vast amounts of power, result in consequences which are ecologically disastrous. The cries from the economic and political spheres for affordable power to sustain high rates of growth and consumption seem to have outweighed these ecological considerations. This paper will explore some of the reasons for the extensive government and industry support for hydro projects as well as the motivation behind the opposition which they encounter. The ecological and social consequences of these projects will be examined. The Churchill-Nelson Hydro Diversion Project, which has been in operation since the 1970's (Waldram 1988:119), will serve as the focus for this paper, however, brief references to other Canadian hydro projects will be made for the sake of comparison.

In the early 1960's the governments of Manitoba and Canada began to explore the overwhelming potential for hydro development in northern Manitoba. Preliminary cost-share studies done by the two levels of government indicated that the Churchill and Nelson rivers had, together, an enormous capacity for the production of cheap electricity (Waldram 1988:118). The only problem with the scheme proposed to harness this capacity was that it would, if carried out, result in the complete flooding of a small village known as South Indian Lake.

Geography

South Indian Lake is located in northern Manitoba in a shallow basin of bedrock on the Churchill River and is approximately 1200 air kilometers north of Winnipeg (Newbury 1984:548; Waldram 1988:115). The lake is actually part of the Churchill River and "...is composed of several irregularily shaped basins separated by narrow channels and islands" (Newbury 1984:551). South Indian is the tenth largest lake in Canada. It is surrounded by extensive boreal forest, but due to the thinness of the soils and the presence of discontinuous permafrost, extensive agriculture is neither practical nor suitable (Waldram 1988:116).

The permafrost soils are roughly 40% water and 60% mineral and organic material (CBC files, Country Canada). Permafrost surrounds most of the lake but does not occur under the basins of the main lake or under its major tributaries because of the waters thermal influence (Newbury 1984:553). The continental climate of the South Indian lake region consists of long cold winters and short cool summers; -50 C is the annual mean temperature (Newbury 1988:552). This was the setting for the establishment of the village of South Indian Lake.

History:

Although it has been difficult to determine the date of the establishment of the village of South Indian Lake, it is known that people have utilized the region's animal resources for food, furs and trade since the early 1800's (Waldram 1988:117). Hunting and trapping has always been a way of life for the people who live there, however, from 1942 until the construction of the hydro project fishing provided the primary economic base for the village.

South Indian Lake was, in fact, northern Manitoba's largest exporter of white fish, with annual catches exceeding 1 million pounds (Newbury 1984:553). The village's Native, non-Native and Metis population had little need or desire for intervention from outside. Unfortunately, the Manitoba Hydro company, together with government, industry and private sectors from southern Manitoba perceived a need for energy which could be fulfilled by disrupting the river system, thus ultimately destroying the lives of these people and the lands and waters upon which they depended.

The Churchill-Nelson Hydro Project

In response to growing demands during the 1960's for an affordable and abundant source of electrical power, Manitoba Hydro was allocated funds for the investigation of the hydroelectric potential of northern river systems (Waldram 1988:118). Plans for a hydro project in the South Indian lake region soon began and a scheme was developed for a water diversion project there. The resulting plan involved completely cutting off the flow of one river and diverting it into a second river. Bocking finds this type of diversion to be the worst form of violence which can be done to the natural flow of a river system (1972:62).

Hydro's plan was simple. A dam was to be erected at the northern outlet of South Indian lake. Because the lake is part of the Churchill River System, this had two effects. First, the flow of the river was blocked 250 miles upstream of Hudson's Bay, and second, with no other available exit, the water flowing into South Indian lake began to flood the banks of the lake and spill out onto the surrounding permafrost landscape (Bocking 1972:63). A channel was then blasted through the land, beginning at a southern point on the lake shore and terminating at the Rat River which leads into the Nelson River via the Burntwood River (Waldram 1988:119). Thus between three quarters and four fifths of the natural northward flow of a river system was forced into a completely different system moving southward. While the Churchill and the Nelson are both very large rivers, the channel created to connect them is relatively much smaller (Manitoba Environmental Council 1973:40).

It was 1966 when Manitoba's premier Duff Roblin announced that this project was ready for government approval and even though the planning phase was far from complete, one Winnipeg newspaper was already referring to the scheme as a "billion dollar dream" (Waldram 1988:120). Jobs would be created, Manitoba's industry and consumers would enjoy cheaper electricity and Canada's trading position with the United States could improve through the exportation of surplus power (Waldram 1988:119; CBC files, Country Canada 1989). The Churchill-Nelson Hydro Project was to be the largest such project of it's time, making the economic and political benefits irresistible. Government popularity would soar as industry expanded, jobs would be created and the low cost of hydro power would drop even lower. The benefits were indeed plentiful, but Manitoba Hydro went one step further by suggesting that the project was economically necessary. At the Manitoba Environment Council's Special Meeting Chris Goodwin, one of Hydro's representatives, noted that "the lower Nelson (river) is the largest resource we have to produce electricity. Any other energy sources we must import. We have virtually no coal, oil or gas" (1973:3). The diversion, it was argued, would guarantee that present and future electrical energy requirements would be met. Time and money would simply be wasted by considering alternatives.

Manitoba Hydro did not recognize that flooding of South Indian Lake would result in the disruption of a village of 900 individuals who depended on the lake. It is also known that the lake would suffer ecological damage. Manitoba Hydro was, however, able to answer concerns such as these. For example, it was to be the responsibility of Manitoba Hydro to finance and compensate for any buildings that needed to be moved or rebuilt and for loss of income due to disruption of fishing. The correction of any resulting destruction of fish and wildlife habitats was also to be Hydro's responsibility (Manitoba Environmental Council's Special Meeting 1973:5 & 6).

While it was clear that the majority of Manitobans would benefit from the diversion, it was equally clear that the people of South Indian Lake would have to make sacrifices. In spite of these realities, it became obvious to some that most of the people and government of Manitoba really knew nothing about the effects which this project would have on South Indian Lake. George Bowman, of the Manitoba Development Agency was quoted as saying "Certainly nobody...can be quite sure of what is going to happen. I think all of us that are reasonable will know that there must be some fish in the lake, and it's going to be a bigger lake so it should be able to carry more fish" (Waldram 1988:124). The absurdity of this statement was albeit somewhat exaggerated, typical of the logic put forth in defense of the plans for this project. Clearly, the pending destruction of the northern landscapes or the lives of its inhabitants were not given much priority. In fact, the then Deputy Minister of the Manitoba Development Authority had the attitude that "...the communities of native people that exist throughout Manitoba...(and) Canada have no future..."unless projects such as this one solve "...the problems of the remote indian settlement..." (ibid:125).

In 1968, Manitoba Hydro's application for its license to commence building was made public and "protests or obligations" were invited (ibid:125).

The Project's Setting

Long before Hydro's application was made public, interest and concern over the project were high. Manitobans had become increasingly aware that similar projects such as the Grand Rapids Dam and the James Bay Project were the cause of human, social and ecological degradation.

In 1960, the Grand Rapids Project was officially announced and was to be the first phase of a massive scheme designed to harness the province's most powerful northern rivers. The Churchill and Nelson rivers were at that time, already selected to be next (Waldram 1988:Ch. 4).

The purpose of the Grand Rapids project was to provide power to industries in Thompson which would in turn stimulate productivity and bring about benefits to all Manitobans. In order to complete the project though, the water levels of a nearby lake were raised about 3.5 meters and the Indian and Metis community of Chemawawin was completely submerged (ibid:Ch 4). In compensation, the entire village was rebuilt at a new location known as Easterville. The new site was however, economically and physically depressed in comparison to the original one (ibid:176).

Another example of a hydroelectric project that has caused degradation is the James Bay Project of Quebec. When it was first announced in 1971, it was said to be for the general and public interests of the people of Quebec. The disruption of the Indian people and lands within the affected region were to be simply regarded as small but necessary sacrifices for the benefit of the majority.

The James Bay Project involved the damming and diverting of five major river systems in Quebec. It has had serious and negative impacts on the surrounding landscapes as well as the six to seven thousand Indian people who live there. It is estimated that "Four thousand square miles of forest and many tens of thousands of miles of productive shoreline have drowned" (Bocking 1972:64-65). Many animals have also been decimated. In countless ways, the outcome of these three projects has been disastrous. One major difference is that unlike the peoples of South Indian Lake and Grand Rapids, those in James Bay have not lost complete control of their traditional lands.

Responses to the Project

For many reasons, much controversy surrounded the Churchill-Nelson Project and by 1969 it had not yet been assured that the areas involved would not suffer damage. Due to demands for environmental impact studies, the then Deputy Minister of Mines and Natural Resources and Chairperson of Manitoba Hydro commissioned the University of Manitoba to "appraise the problem and suggest the various aspects of it that should be examined later..." (Waldram 1988:120).

By January, 1967, the Reconnaissance Study (or Duckworth Report) was submitted. In brief, the report's primary recommendation was that the level of South Indian Lake not be raised at all and that existing available alternatives to flooding be considered. The authors feared that Hydro would ultimately succeed in creating "...the biggest man made swamp in the world" (ibid:122).

In June, two years later, hope for the lake, its surroundings and the people who lived there seemed to be in sight. The New Democratic Party won the provincial election over the Conservatives: a victory which is said to be at least partially due to the new premier Ed Schreyer's promise to reconsider the Churchill diversion (Bocking 1972:64). The new government shut down the project, reconsidered its value and determined that the province could not afford to cancel it altogether. However, instead of the original "high-level" diversion which would cause 10 meters of flooding, a "low level" diversion was suggested which would only allow between three and five meters of flooding. Bocking has referred to this as a meaningless gesture since it was known that the greatest damage would be done by the first few feet of higher water (1972:64). The new scheme was therefore not worthy of praise and the people of South Indian Lake became suspicious that the lower level flooding would only be the first step in the destruction of their lake and livelihoods (ibid: 64).

In spite of all the controversy and opposition created by the Churchill-Nelson Hydro Project, the New Democratic Party was reelected in 1973. Construction of the diversion continued and the people of South Indian Lake found themselves with little recourse. Money for legal fees was largely unavailable and impact studies opposing the project were either still underway or had been completed and rejected. One report had been accepted and it argued that "...northern Native people were in transition from some kind of primitive past to a technological present..."; they were nothing more than "...anachronisms in the present age of technology..." (Waldram 1988:121). The hydro project was therefore seen as a catalyst which would move the people foreward in time by breaking up their traditional ways of life.

Results of the Diversion

The Churchill-Nelson river systems promised a generating capacity of 6.14 Megawatts of hydroelectric power (Manitoba Hydro, 1985). This large scale project, now in operation for twelve years, was deemed necessary by both industry and government for many reasons, a few of which have been examined above. It is ironic that in economic terms, the province of Manitoba has actually lost rather than gained from the project. This is especially true when the long term degradation of the land and resulting consequences (such as the economic and social losses suffered by the northern people) are considered. From the perspective of the people of South Indian Lake, the project has clearly been a disaster. Interviews with many South Indian Lake residents were conducted by the Canadian Broadcasting Corporation (CBC) in the late summer of 1989 for a documentary program called Country Canada and the overwhelming feelings I get from reading these are ones of sadness and frustration. These are the sentiments expressed by the people of South Indian Lake.

William Dysart, a fisherman in the village said that he used to haul in 15 to 16 tubs of fish per day using between 6 to 10 nets. Since the water in the lake has been high due to the diversion he must now use between 20 and 40 nets and can only catch 7 or 8 tubs of fish. He said that the spawning grounds have been damaged because erosion has covered them with sediments and mud. The fish must now try to live in water conditions which are not good for their survival. William believed that their food supply must also be bad. While opening fish to be dressed he and other fishermen have found many fish which had eaten the fir from the trees that fall in the water. He thought many fish must be dying from eating this. Factors such as these have made fishing an unviable livelihood and Manitoba Hydro is seen to be their cause.

R.E. Hecky, et al. of the Department of Fisheries and Oceans, Freshwater Institute, have shown through their research that the claims made by William Dysart are very accurate. The researchers have determined that because the diversion has added excess waters to the lake that are warmer than those naturally found in the lake, erosion of the permafrost soil along the shoreline has occured very quickly. These soils are about 40% ice and they melt quickly when warmed. This has caused the remaining minerals, organic matter and overlying vegetation to collapse into the lake (CBC files for Country Canada). These sediments, suspended in the water of the lake, affect the lake's inhabitants in many ways. First, the lake now contains more mercury than before due to the shoreline erosion. Visibility in the lake is reduced making it more difficult for the fish population to feed successfully. This has led the fish to seek out more favorable feeding areas. As well, the increasing concentrations of silt and clay in the water are covering spawning beds, thereby reducing the chances of survival of the whitefish eggs (Hecky, et.al. 1984:732).

All commercial fish species show increases in mercury concentrations, particularly in their muscle tissues. This has brought about a sharp decline of their market quality. In the food chain, mercury is absorbed by the zooplankton (a fish tropic level) which the fish eat. Since the fish are in the second tropic level of this particular food chain, they concentrate the mercury by approximately 90%. Even a small amount of mercury is regarded as undesirable. Tragically, the mercury problem seems to be getting worse. Hydro's diversion continues to raise and lower lake levels each fall and spring, allowing for continued soil erosion and the consequent leaching of more mercury into the water. Mercury levels have in fact been so high that fish sent for testing to the Freshwater Institute have failed to pass inspection (CBC files for Country Canada).

Not surprisingly, the people of South Indian Lake are now afraid to eat the fish. Some people are even suspicious that the increased numbers of miscarriages in pregnant women as well as increased rates of alcoholism and premature greying are related to the mercury problems (CBC files for Country Canada). Besides the collapse of the fishing industry, South Indian Lake has suffered in other ways as well. John B. Moose, a resident who has fished in the lake for the past 49 years, was asked by CBC to share some of his insights. According to him, the livelihoods of his people have been spoiled because of the way the level of the diversion waters fluctuate from season to season in a very unnatural way. As a result, trapping animals like the beaver is impossible because they end up freezing to death.

...even the ducks have disappeared...feeding grounds are all spoiled and the fish are going somewhere else...everything, moose, deer, they don't stick around here anymore...you can go eighty miles from here to the lake and you'll find maybe two places where you can park a boat. The rest of the places are ruined, sticks are piled up on the shoreline and the shoreline is dead. Even the islands are underwater. They should mark where the islands used to be...you must be careful with your motor now 'cause there's lots of sticks in the lake bottom...

John Moose was brought up on the lake and claims to know it very well. He says that when the people from Hydro came to the village, he tried to warn them of the consequences of flooding the lake but the men wouldn't listen. The people of Hydro said they knew more than he did. In the long run, the foresight of John Moose and many others has proven to be correct.

Dr. Robert Newbury of the University of Manitoba's Civil Engineering Department was one of is projects strongest opponents. He refers to it as "...the largest, most destructive project in North America right now in terms of reservoirs" (CBC files for Country Canada). As he sees it, Hydro simply designed a diversion of outrageous proportions and then built it on a northern landscape. The problem, however, was that their experience with northern landscapes was very limited. It had been suggested right from the project's beginning that an experimental flooding be done in a small piece of permafrost just to see what would happen. There was a great deal of excitement surrounding the project. Momentum was building very quickly, and unfortunately, the experiment just didn't get done. The project now stands as an example of a "major blunder in northern planning...and is a world class embarrassment" (CBC files for Country Canada).

Newbury has recognized that the fabric of the landscape and the fabric of the village were essentially one and the same until Hydro destroyed them. He says that the "...people are still there but the fabric of living there is no longer there" (CBC files for Country Canada). He estimates that it may take centuries for the land to restabilize and criticizes Hydro for its ludicrous suggestion that five years would be a sufficient amount of time.

As for the village of South Indian Lake, the Manitoba government proudly boasts that all problems have been solved. A new road was built, bungalows with electrical power erected, a shopping center and town hall were built and a landscaped town square completed the new townsite. The real problems, however, remain. The people of that newly constructed village have little or nothing to do but to sit in the new houses, use their electricity and run up bills they cannot afford to pay (CBC files for Country Canada). The government has offered these people mediocre technological solutions to ensure their physical survival but has done nothing about their mental survival or moral outlook on the world. Manitoba Hydro has removed them from a living landscape and there is no technological fix for that.

Residents of South Indian Lake say they feel bitter about what has happened. They say that the things they loved the most (the land and waters) have been destroyed forever. The people knew that Hydro had been studying what would happen if the lake were to be flooded and they knew what the outcome would be. "They knew, but they were after the high water for Hydro purposes. That was the main goal no matter what. They used to come here and say that our lives would be a lot better with hydro power. I think we would've been a lot better off if we would've been left alone. We could've done without hydro power, that's for sure" (CBC files Country Canada).

Conclusion

Through the close examination of one hydroelectric diversion project, it has been shown that while short term economic and political gains may be attractive, long term results can be very costly. This is especially true for the northern villages which are directly and profoundly affected by such projects. In Canada, very few hydrological projects were preceded by impact assessments even though ecological disaster has usually been recognized as unavoidable. It is amazing that the damming and diverting of rivers continues when ecological risks are high. But governments have managed to outweigh such issues by appealing to the "public interest" (Waldram 1988:172).

Garrett Hardin, in his Tragedy of the Commons essay, has pointed out that the promotion of public interest is quite impossible because it assumes that decisions reached individually, by a political leader for example, will, in fact, be the best decisions for an entire society. In the case of South Indian Lake, Manitoba's premier decided that the Churchill-Nelson Hydro Project would benefit most, if not all, people of the province. As was made clear throughout this paper, this was far from true. What has been true is that "There is a political imperative and...an imperative which drives huge crown corporations. If those two imperatives meet and there is a community of interest, they will find a way of achieving what tends to be a shared objective" (CBC files for Country Canada). In the past, this has usually been done with total disregard for the ecosystems which are found within the community of shared interest.

For the sake of the future, we must stop treating the northern resources of water, minerals, forests, etc. like packages which are sitting up on some shelf waiting to be brought down to be 'developed.' An understanding of those resources and how they work together must be found so that even after they are utilized, they can continue working together in a balanced manner. As Robert Newberry has argued

"...these northern places where the so called development projects are occurring may become more amenable in the future as the climate changes and agricultural lands evolve...and as we develop them over the next century, we may find that those are desirable places to live...". Our short sightedness may, however, make this impossible. The destruction of natural ecosystems for the sake of instant profit must stop because in the long run, it will cost much more than bargained for.

Greg Young-Ing

Identifying First Nation Environmental Flash Points

(Excerpt)

(Excerpt from a paper originally written for the Assembly of First Nations' Committee on the Environment in 1990 as part of the Assembly's response to the Government of Canada's proposed environmental agenda known as the Green Plan.)

INTRODUCTION

This paper was written in response to what First Nations see as the Federal Government's attempt to downplay the role and concerns of our people in the formulation of the Green Plan. In our view, this is yet another saga in the ongoing history of the breakdown in proper relations between First Nations and the Federal Government. Whether there is hope for improving that relationship under the current Federal regime remains to be seen; however, our experience to date with the Green Plan will certainly not help unless some serious effort is made to respond to our rights, concerns and needs.

Our hopes were raised when the Federal Government announced its intent to establish a "partnership" with Aboriginal peoples in the formulation of the Green Plan. We saw this as an opportunity to gain recognition of our inherent right to protect our environment. Now, unfortunately, as the consultation phases of the Green Plan formulation draw to a close, we find ourselves struggling to respond to what has been a shallow and unrealistic "consultation process."

When the Federal Government released "A Framework for Discussion on the Environment," announcing their plan for soliciting input into the formulation of the Green Plan, we were delighted to see that the document opened with a quote from Chief Seattle. We were further encouraged by the following statement in the Framework:

> "Canada's aboriginal peoples are often the first to experience changes made to the natural environment by human activities. Those changes have sometimes threatened their traditional and close relationship to the land."
>
> The Government is committed to cooperative efforts with Canada's aboriginal people to address environmental issues of concern to them. For example, the Government is considering the establishment of an environmental advisory committee composed of representatives of First Nations to ensure that federal initiatives are sensitive to the concerns of native

> native peoples and supportive of their efforts to manage their own affairs. The Government will also consult with aboriginal peoples about other possible initiatives, including measures to support activities of natives that enhance or protect the environment and a special native component to the Government youth employment initiatives."

In spite of the appeal of this statement, in our view, the actual Framework contains no mechanism that allows for meaningful First Nations' input into the formulation and implementation of the Green Plan.

Although some First Nations were invited to participate in the series of "discussions" held across the country as part of the developmental stages of the Green Plan, very few did. Nearly all First Nation communities and organizations have no environmental expertise on staff. Additional burdens were placed upon the regular staff to attend sessions, for which they are not adequately prepared.

After four and a half months of hype about "consultation", the First Nations are still waiting for a true opportunity to do so. Once again, we fear that we will be listened to - but not heard.

PURPOSE

Through outlining the circumstances of various First Nation "environmental flash points", the information presented in this paper will indicate First Nations' environmental concerns warrant a much more significant role than is being acknowledged. In support of this argument, brief overviews of specific examples where First Nations have been severely impacted in relation to the issues identified in the Green Plan will be provided.

BACKGROUND

First Nations have always had great concern for the welfare of the future generations and the condition of the natural elements in our territories which we will pass on to them. For our part, we have always recognized the delicate relationship between a healthy people and a clean environment. For thousands of years, before European settlement and colonization, the First Nations' holistic philosophy of sustainable development through long term planning and appropriate technology had nurtured a land where there was virtually no permanent environmental destruction or deterioration due to human carelessness and ignorance.

Our witnessing the arrival of newcomers into our territories, and the subsequent environmental destruction waged throughout the North American continent, has only served to deepen our concern. Given that newcomers onto our territories have almost obliterated certain aspects of our environment beyond the possibility of any hope of recovery, First Nations should at least have an opportunity to establish a remedial and new relationship with Canada that recognizes our inherent knowledge and ability to protect a healthy ecosystem.

This principle is recognized in the United Nations commissioned and Canadian Government endorsed Bruntland Report which states:

> "Some communities - so-called indigenous or tribal peoples - remain isolated because of such factors as physical barriers to communication or marked differences in social or cultural practices... The isolation of many such people has meant the preservation of a traditional way of life in close harmony with the natural environment...
>
> These communities are the repositories of vast accumulations of traditional knowledge and experience that links humanity with its ancient origins... The larger society could learn a great deal from their traditional skills in sustainably managing very complex ecological systems."

JURISDICTIONAL CONSIDERATIONS

First Nations not only deserve to have their knowledge and concerns incorporated into the Green Plan, but consideration must be given to the jurisdictional uncertainty that we find ourselves in today. Traditionally, our territories usually follow natural boundaries such as those delineated by mountain ranges, forests and waterways.

Artificial boundaries imposed by federal, provincial and municipal governments usually do not follow natural boundaries and have created a situation where different parts of traditional territories and even reserves are under different sets of regulations.

First Nations now find themselves in jurisdictional chaos due to overlapping and competing regulatory authorities. Meanwhile, unscrupulous developers see opportunities in the gaps caused by these competing authorities in addition to inadequate law and lack of clarification in the Indian Act. As a result, increasing instances of proposed or existing environmentally questionable development are thrust upon Native communities without their being fully aware of the legal and environmental consequences.

Constitutionally, First Nations are clearly a federal responsibility while, at the same time, many hunting, fishing and conservation regulations are provincial. Other contradictions arise in cases where hunting and fishing rights are recognized in treaties, but are in conflict with federal or provincial laws, or with legislation such as the Migratory Birds Convention Act.

There are also serious problems in Canadian policy and Canadian law. A major conflict lies in the fact that Section 35 of the Constitution recognizes Aboriginal rights which the Courts have, on several occasions, defined to include hunting and fishing rights. At the same time, First Nation people are required to obtain hunting and fishing licences from provinces and have conservation regulations imposed on them.

Additional jurisdictional complications arise in cases where reserves are located within the boundaries of national or provincial parks. It is also unclear how provincial and municipal standards on matters like pollution emissions, land fill sites and incinerator monitoring should be applied to federal reserve land. To further complicate matters, Canada seems uncertain about the application of existing federal legislation and regulations (i.e., The Canadian Environmental Protection Act) to reserve lands.

To summarize, there are several environmental issues confronted by First Nations that fall into a jurisdictional limbo. To avoid further complications, these matters need to be given careful consideration in the formulation of the Green Plan. As far as we can see, they are not.

GREEN PLAN IDENTIFIED CATEGORIES

The Federal Government's Framework for the Green Plan segregates actions needed into the following categories and sub-categories:

A. Environmental Stresses (Toxic Substances, Waste Management, Environmental Emergencies, the Health Dimension)

B. The Global Commons (Atmospheric Change, Global Warming, Ozone Depletion, Acid Rain, Air Quality, and Toxic Pollutants, Water)

C. Sustaining Our Renewable Resources (Agriculture, Forests, Fisheries)
D. Preserving Ecological and Heritage Resources (National Parks and Historic sites Wildlife)
E. Protecting the Arctic Environment

FIRST NATION ENVIRONMENTAL FLASH POINTS

A. ENVIRONMENTAL STRESSES

TOXIC SUBSTANCES

Prior to the arrival of settlers, toxic substances in North America were created naturally or by Aboriginal peoples in the course of their daily lives in such small quantities that they were non-threatening. Now many First Nations find themselves in situations where, because they are often located in isolated areas, their territories are targeted for resource development and the disposal of waste matter from another society. Although First Nations rarely benefit from profits made through so-called industrial and municipal development, they often suffer the consequences of industry's negligence.

Uranium Mining Near Wollaston Lake

The Hatchet Lake Chipewyan and Metis people live in an isolated community on the south eastern edge of Wollaston Lake in northern Saskatchewan. They have been dependent on fishing along with moose hunting and trapping since settling in the village in the 1950's. Since the 1970's, Eldorado Nuclear Limited and other corporations have set up uranium extraction plants on lakes in the immediate area. In the 1980's, it had become one of the highest uranium extracting areas in the world with what was once the worlds largest uranium mine at Key Lake and smaller plants at Rabbit Lake, Cluff Lake and Collin's Bay.

It became apparent that the general health of the people in the area had severely declined since the mining began, and the Chipewans had strong suspicions that radioactive waste from the uranium mining in the area had affected the moose, the water and the fish. These suspicions were intensified in 1985 when the Atomic Energy Control Board initiated a case against Eldorado Nuclear Limited in the Saskatchewan Provincial Court, charging that they had broken conditions of the mine operating licence by releasing high levels of radioactive waste. The provincial Attorney General responded by issuing a "stay", ordering the case not be heard.

The Chipewan people and their supporters showed their frustration in 1985 by staging an eight day blockade of one of the mining roads leading to the Rabbit Lake and Collin's Bay uranium mines.

In November of 1989, the Chemco uranium plant at Wollaston Lake spilled 2 million litres of untreated water contaminated with radium 226 into Collins Creek, just upstream from the river which runs by the Hatchet Lake Reserve. The leak was caused by a broken valve in a pipe which went undetected flowing for 16 hours. To date the community has not received any compensation or response to appeals for a formal inquiry.

Toxic Waste Problems in Mohawk Territory of Kahnawake

In 1986, at the Mohawk Territory of Kahnawake near Montreal, Quebec, a major fire broke out at one of the four major landfill sites in Kahnawake. All four of the sites were located on privately owned reserve land. The Kahnawake Environmental Protection Committee (KEPC) was formed soon afterwards.

After the fire all the landfill sites were closed down and the KEPC managed to have Environment Canada and Environment Quebec commission various studies. One study found that 1 in 2 water wells - the only source of water in the outlying areas of the reserve - contain dangerously high levels of sulphur and fluoride. The KEPC had also acquired funds from the Department of Indian Affairs and Environment Canada to monitor the level of toxins in ground water near the landfill sites. Those funds were recently cut off.

WASTE MANAGEMENT

Landfill Site Near Bonaparte Reserve

The Shuswaps on Bonaparte Reserve near Cache Creek, British Columbia, are fighting for the closure of a landfill site situated just off the reserve boundaries but within their traditional territories, where the Wastec company disposes of garbage from the city of Vancouver. Since 1988, when the land fill site began operating, several different kinds of toxic chemicals have been dumped into the ground.

The Shuswaps have suspicions that a lot of the landfill waste comes from a toxic waste plant in Cache Creek. Recently they have learned that hot fuel loaded with PCB's has been dumped into the site. It is unclear whether provincial and federal regulations are being followed, or whether a proper environmental assessment was conducted. The Bonaparte Shuswaps are not only concerned about the effect of the toxic waste on the air and soil, but also that the ground water around the landfill is being contaminated and filtering into the nearby Fraser River upstream from the Reserve and its fishing sites. Existing policy and legislative frameworks cannot address these matters.

ENVIRONMENTAL EMERGENCIES

Oil Spill Disaster Strikes in Nuu-chah-nulth Territory

In December, 1988, Nuu-chah-nulth people on the west coast of Vancouver Island began to notice oil washing up onto the shores of their territories. Days earlier a barge owned by Sause Brothers Ocean Towing of Coos Bay, Oregon, had leaked 875,000 litres of crude oil just off the Washington coast. It was later determined that officials in Washington ordered the ship to go further out to sea when it started leaking, to avoid spilling into their harbour, thus causing the spill to spread further across the coast.

The Provincial Government of B.C. responded immediately by declaring that the spill was a federal responsibility. However, it was not until January 9th that federal officials inspected the shoreline and announced that resources would be made available for the clean-up.

Meanwhile, the Nuu-chal-nuth Tribal Council (NTC) had already begun to clean up the oil in their territories themselves. The NTC also hired a professional biologist and divers at their own expense to assess the damage. To date, the spill has cost the NCT over $ 100,000.00 for which they are demanding compensation from the oil company, and the U.S. and Canadian governments.

Of even greater concern to the Nuu-chal-nuth people is the effect of the spill on the marine food chain. Crabs and other shellfish, which are part of the traditional Nuu-chal-nuth diet, have already been found to be contaminated, thus raising fears of contamination and population loss of other seafoods in the area.

Emergency Preparedness for Northern Manitoba Forest Fires

The forest fires that break out in northern Manitoba virtually every summer are a great concern to the many First Nation communities in the area. Not only is there potential for loss of human lives, but traplines, sacred sites, wildlife and entire reserves are placed under the threat of destruction.

One major problem with the ability of the authorities to deal with the forest fires lies in the Manitoba's "fire fighting priority areas". Under this scheme, different areas of the Province are subjected to a priority ranking system which determines how much fire fighting resources, emergency planning, and access to necessary equipment are allotted in the particular area. First Nations are concerned because the ranking system is based primarily on population density.

Consequently, for example, urban centres are ranked high priority areas and remote northern regions are ranked low.

During the 1989 forest fires, based on fears that mechanisms in Manitoba were not in place to adequately respond to the fires, First Nation groups began looking for alternative mechanisms. Out of this effort, they contacted Native firemen across the country and found an overwhelming number of them were willing to be on call to fly into northern Manitoba as part of a special emergency team. Unfortunately, the proposal of having a cross country Native fire fighting team on call was dashed for the time being when it was found that resources would not be provided. The Province of Manitoba said that they would not provide resources because reserves are a federal responsibility, and DIAND also refused to cover the cost of the operation.

THE HEALTH DIMENSION

Mercury Poisoning at Grassy Narrows Reserve

The Ojibway people of Grassy Narrows near Kenora, Ontario, were uprooted by the federal Governments relocation program in the early 1960's. In 1970, while the community was struggling to adjust to foreign living conditions, it was discovered that the English, Wabigoon, and Winnipeg river systems which ran by the new Grassy Narrows Reserve were severely polluted by mercury from the Reed Pulp and Paper Plant upstream. By then, it was too late.

Mercury contamination was found in most of the people in the community, caused undoubtedly from contaminated fish consumption. Several members of the community suffered, and continue to suffer, from symptoms of Minamata disease such as vision deterioration and deformities. It is also likely that many ill effects have thus far gone undetected and may show up in future generations.

People from the neighbouring Whitedog Reserve were also affected by the mercury poisoning, but not to the extent of the people of Grassy Narrows.

Epidemic Spreads Through James Bay Cree Territory

In 1975, the Grand Council of the Crees (of Quebec) signed the first modern day treaty, the James Bay and Northern Quebec Agreement. After five years of trying to implement the Agreement and pressuring the federal and provincial governments to live up to their end of the deal, the Crees were becoming increasingly frustrated.

Each year children and elderly became infected from drinking water contaminated with sewage. Promised sanitation and water projects required under the Treaty had been denied for five years under the pretext that there were insufficient funds. Five of the Cree communities had no sewage or water supply system. Toilets were being run into pits where the ground did not have the capacity to absorb the waste, causing the pits to overflow each spring.

In the Fall of 1980, an epidemic swept through the Cree villages of Fort Rupert and Nemaska. Eight Cree children died during the epidemic from complications related to gastroenteritis, while both the federal and provincial governments denied that any kind of health problem existed. It was only when the media became interested that the resulting embarrassment forced the governments to act. An emergency team of doctors was airlifted to the Cree villages and saw firsthand the consequences of government irresponsibility and neglect. Initially, government officials tried to suppress the medical teams report; but finally, through the insistence of the media, the report was made public. The doctors reported that the epidemic was the direct result of the failure of Canada and Quebec to respect specific provisions in the Agreement.

The tragedy sparked the federal and provincial governments to react to the situation, and all Cree communities in James Bay now have sewage and water systems.

B. THE GLOBAL COMMONS

AIR QUALITY

Whether First Nations communities are located downwind from major industrial sites, near standard burn-and-bury garbage sites, or have Land Range Transport of Airborne Pollutants in place, most have little control or access to information which could empower them to improve their local air quality.

Industrial Emissions Near Mohawk Territory of Kahnawake

The Mohawk territory of Kahnawake is plagued by off-reserve pollutants. The Novalead plant is situated just off the Reserve 150 meters away from the Kahnawake Survival School. The plant breaks down used car batteries and emits noxious fumes. On several occasions a cloud from the plant has descended upon the school, forcing an evacuation of the building. Some children at the school have also suffered unusual coughing and headaches which the Mohawks fear are related to the emissions.

In addition to the Novalead plant, emissions also come from an Associated Steel automobile metal recycling plant and an ICTG propane plant. The Kahnawake Environmental Protection Committee has recently responded by securing funds from Environment Canada and Health and Welfare Canada to do an ambient air study in the area.

WATER

Most of the problems experienced by First Nations, regarding water, have centred around such issues as pollution, flooding, hydro electric projects, the right to resources in and under water and issues of jurisdiction and responsibility. There are also a compounding number of cases where problems arise due to seepage from dump and landfill sites on or near reserves, agricultural and municipal drainage and the effects of acid rain.

Mohawks of the Bay of Quinte Water Quality Study

Approximately 10% of the homes on the Tyendinaga Reserve use water from a nearby water treatment plant. The remainder use water supplied by wells. This well water runs out of the Bay of Quinte of Lake Ontario.

Concern over the rising level of pollution in Lake Ontario, and indeed in all of the Great Lakes, led the Mohawks to initiate a water study in 1990. Initial findings have shown that, as the Mohawks suspected, the majority of wells contain high bacteria levels and are not fit for drinking.

Extensive Flooding on Mount Currie Reserve

An example of the problems caused by imposing the non-Indian way of life upon Indians is the flooding of certain parts of Mt. Currie Indian Reserve in 1983. In the fall of that year, the overflow from the Lil'wat River spread across a large portion of the reserve, covering the Bands graveyard, destroying several houses and forcing evacuations.

It was later came out that the flooding was largely attributed to extensive clear cut logging upriver in Meager Creek. There large portions of forested mountain sides had been taken out leaving no root systems to hold soil onto the mountainside. As a result, mountain springs, rain water, land slides, contributed to the flooding of the River.

The Mount Currie Lil'wats remain legitimately concerned because they continue to live in a flood plain between the Lil'wat and Bikenhead rivers where clear-cut logging continues.

Ingenika Band Without Compensation for 21 Years After Flooding and Attempted Relocation

The isolated Ingenika community of Sekani Indians in the northern interior of British Columbia number about two hundred. They are semi-nomadic people dependent on hunting, trapping and fishing in the valley surrounding Williston Lake.

The community was given no consultation in the mid 60's when the WAC Bennett hydro dam was built in a reservoir on Williston Lake. Shortly afterwards, community members noticed the water level in the lake slowly climbing up the valley. No warning was given to the community when the hydro dam was filled in 1967. Extensive flooding spread across the valley destroying the community's homes and camps a year later.

After the disaster the Ingenika Band was relocated onto a newly established reserve outside of their traditional territory. The community responded by abandoning the Reserve and returning to their Ingenika Point.

When they returned they found their traditional territory in a deplorable state. Huge mud and dust flats had formed along the Lake's shoreline caused by B.C. Hydro draining down the dam. They could no longer fish the lake because it was filled with dead trees which tangled their nets. The water level had also risen so high up the valley that trees were submerged underwater and would occasionally uproot and come quickly shooting to the surface damaging or destroying boats. The lake had also become contaminated with waste from pulp and paper mills located upstream the MacKenzie river. To compound matters, there was no drinkable water for eight kilometres, no electricity and no road access. In addition, logging started to come into the area, threatening to destroy traplines and hunting areas.

The community lived under these conditions for 21 years when finally a settlement was reached in 1989. The agreement was reached between the Federal Government, the Provincial Government of B.C., B.C. Hydro and the Ingenika Sekanis. Under the agreement the community receives financial compensation, a 3,000 acre reserve and a school.

C. SUSTAINING OUR RENEWABLE RESOURCES FORESTS

Teme-Aguma Anishnawbe Territory Targeted by Logging

The Teme-Aguma Anishnawbe people have lived in n'Daki-Menan, their sacred homeland in Northern Ontario, for at least 6,000 years. Since European encroachment onto their territories in the late 1800's, they have never signed a treaty or in any other way surrendered title to any portion of their territories. The Teme-Aguma Anishnawbe have economic, political, social and spiritual practices which are inseparably connected to their heavily forested territory.

Logging began in the 1920's and all season logging roads began the 1960's. However, the major forestry problems began in 1972 when the Ontario Government proposed an 80 million dollar resort in an area held to be most sacred to the Tema-Aguma Anishnawbe. Since that time, the people have embarked on a concerted effort to protect the ancient white pine and other trees in their homelands from the logging barons.

This struggle came to a head in 1988 when the Ontario Government decided to extend logging further into the heart of n'Daki-Menan and, again, into another sacred area. It was then that the Tema-Aguma Anishnawbe reacted by erecting road blocks in defence of their territory.

The Algonquins of Barriere Lake Oppose Quebec Forestry Regime

The Algonguins of Barriere Lake living in La Verendrye Wildlife

Reserve in southwestern Quebec have been subjected to intense logging in their traditional territories which has severely disrupted their traditional land-based economy. Unfortunately, despite the Barriere Lake community's repeated calls for a moratorium on the signing of Forestry Management Agreements (FMA); for the area, the signing of agreements went ahead in 1989.

The FMAs are twenty-five year agreements, with five year extensions every five years if the holder conforms to obligations. They are the result of closed-door negotiations between the Quebec government and the forestry companies. The Agreements are basically geared towards ensuring an adequate supply of wood for the company mills. They allocate to the holder an annual volume of wood to be harvested for each of the twenty-five years of the agreement, and confer upon the holder the right to obtain an annual forest management permit upon approval of the annual forest management plan.

Research done by the Algonquins has concluded that with the FMAs, based as they are on the current land use designations in the agreements, leave little hope for adequate protection of the wildlife, aesthetic and recreational values of the La Verendrye Wildlife Reserve - not to mention the future of the Algonquin land-based economy.

In addition to the research, the people of Barriere Lake have been working to bring the Canadian and Quebec governments to the table to participate in the development and implementation of a conservation strategy. The main stumbling block in these efforts to date is Quebec's lack of will to compromise with regard to the FMAs.

Given recent failed attempts to arrive at a reasonable compromise with the Quebec minister responsible for forests, the community set up blockades on logging roads in their Territories.

FISHERIES

BC Chiefs Alliance Challenge Twin Tracking Proposal in Court

Since at least 1984, the First Nations along Fraser, Thompson and North Thompson Rivers have been fighting to prevent Canadian National Railway's proposal to construct a second track along tracks which run by the rivers. To this end, 36 Chiefs in the area formed an alliance and commenced litigation against C.N.R. in order to prevent the double tracking. The major issue of contention is that the construction of the second track would require the dumping of massive amounts of rip rap into the shorelines, thus further destroying the fish spawning areas.

Git'skan Wet'suwet'en Assertion of Fishing Rights

The Git'skan Wet'suwet'en people live in north central British Columbia. Their territories include most of the upper watershed of the Skeena River in addition to parts of the adjacent Nass and Fraser River. The salmon fisheries of the Skeena River system are the economic base of the Git'skan and Wet'suwet'en people. Traditionally, these fisheries are organized on the basis of a management system in which final authority rests with the Hereditary Chiefs.

In the late 19th century, an industrial salmon fishery was established at the mouth of the Skeena. At that time, the Canadian government unilaterally asserted management authority over Skeena fishery resources. Since then, there has been continuing conflict between Indian and federal authorities.

In 1977, the Git'ksan - Wet'suwet'en Tribal Council (GWTC) began acting on behalf the Hereditary Chiefs in attempting to resolve the conflict. As part of this effort, the Tribal Council has developed fishery management proposals based on cultural and biological research and has mapped out a political strategy combining litigation and negotiation.

The GWTC completed a six year study of the Indian fishery and other Skeena fisheries in 1985. Through the proposals which came out of the study, the chiefs acknowledge that the fish migrate outside of their jurisdiction; and, therefore, there is a need to co-ordinate management with those outside the territory.

Based on the principle of coordinated management, the GWTC are presently holding negotiations with the Department of Indian Affairs, the Department of Fisheries and Oceans (DFO) and other First Nation groups in the area. A fisheries agreement is presently being worked out between the GWTC, the Lake Babine Band and the Tsimshan Tribal Council. Fisheries proposals are also included as part the GWTC Self-Government negotiations being held with the Federal Government. In addition, the Hereditary Chiefs are waiting for the Supreme Court of British Columbia decision on their right to ownership and jurisdiction over resources within their traditional territories.

The Nicole Case recognizes the Git'skan Wet'suwet'en right to fish irrespective of conservation measures; which, together with the Sparrow decision, has given the GWTC increased negotiating power in meetings with DFO. In recent discussions with DFO, the GWTC has taken the position that DFO regulations do not apply to them and therefore, they are refusing to acquire fishing permits. In addition,

GWTC has been asked to adhere to conservation regulations by respecting a three day closure of the Coho Salmon fishery, to which they have also refused.

D. PRESERVING ECOLOGICAL AND HERITAGE RESOURCES

NATIONAL PARKS

The only section of the National Park Act referring to "Native people" is section 11(1). It specifies that certain areas of the Yukon or the Northwest Territories may be set aside as a reserve for a national park of Canada, pending a settlement in respect of any right, title or interest of the people of Native origin. In addition, this Section establishes that - with the exception of Native traditional hunting, fishing and trapping activities - the National Parks Act applies on any reserve within the boundaries of the Park.

The Parks Canada Policy published in 1985 specifies the conditions for the creation of National Park Reserves. These are interim measures with temporary boundaries until such time as land claims are settled. According to the Policy, in order to create a National Park Reserve, the "Comprehensive Land Claim" must have been filed by the concerned native groups and must have been accepted for negotiation by the Federal Government.

Once the land claims have been settled between the claimant group and the Federal Government, the official boundaries of the new national park are set according to the provisions of the Agreement. The Park boundaries can also be set out in negotiations outside of the land claims process.

According to Section 1.3.13 of the Policy, prior to formal establishment of new national parks, the parties will be negotiating an agreement creating a joint management regime between Native communities and the park's administration. This bilateral agreement is supposedly for the planning and management of the park, including fishing, hunting and trapping activities. Subsection III of the Policy specifies that in newly established national parks, the treaty rights of Indian people and those rights recognized in land claims settlements will be honoured.

Co-management Plan For The Mingan Montagnais Band

The aforementioned provisions of the National Park Act and the Parks Canada Policy did not appear to do much for the Mingan

Montagnais. Being located in the Mingan Archipelago National Park Reserve, the First Nation community has been negotiating with Parks Canada, without success, for four years trying to establish a role in the management of wildlife and its harvesting, but to no avail.

There have even been a few cases where Montagnais people were prosecuted for fishing or hunting without licences. As this case has shown, the so-called "co-management regime" can turn out to be a structure giving virtually no power nor decision-making opportunities to Native people in the management of resources despite their having been living there first. It appears that, despite the National Park Act and Policy pertaining to First Nations, in reality the Minister and Park administrators merely pay lip service to First Nation concerns and then unilaterally make decisions on wildlife management policies in the Park themselves.

HERITAGE SITES

Mt. Currie and Lytton Indian Communities Join Forces to Protect Stein Valley

The Mt. Currie and Lytton Indian communities in the interior British Columbia have united in the fight to protect the Stein Valley from proposed logging and industrial developments. The Stein Valley is the traditional territory of the Lytton Nlaka'pamux and Mt. Currie Lilo'wat people.

The Valley contains numerous petroglyph sites, burial grounds and remains from ancient villages. These sites were left by their ancestors, and are of great spiritual, cultural and historical significance. With regard to the environmental concerns, protection of the Valley is important because the 420 square mile wilderness area contains the last unlogged, undeveloped watershed in southern British Columbia. The healthy ecosystem is centred around a clean river, an ancient growth forest, alpine meadows and numerous glacier-fed lakes, as well as the many species of wildlife.

Logging and other industrial development in the Stein Valley has been steady over the last decade, but threatened to increase in 1985 after corporations began extensive surveying of the lower canyon. Although an agreement between the two Indian communities and the Provincial Government has forced a moratorium on logging for the time being, it is feared that the valley remains under threat. In order to protect the valley, Mt. Currie, Lytton and environmental groups have jointly formed the Stein Valley Preservation Fund, which proposes to have aboriginal title recognized through the creation of the Stein Valley Tribal Heritage Park.

WILDLIFE

First Nations' concerns with wildlife are mostly related to issues such as conservation, hunting rights, jurisdiction and conflicts with Canadian Law.

First Nations find it ironic that federal and provincial conservation regulations are imposed on them when it was clearly the carelessness of Canadian people - and not First Nations - which has caused the disruption, depletion and extinction of various species. Prior to European settlement there was no evidence of mass species loss or depletion, except that which occurred through the natural and evolutionary process.

Low-Level Flight Testing Disrupts Caribou Herds in Innu Territory

The Innu call their land "Natassinan" which, on a modern day map of Canada, covers parts of Labrador and north eastern Quebec. They are among the most isolated First Nation communities who have been able maintain their traditions. In most Innu communities, the lifestyle revolves heavily around the caribou herds in their territory. Like several other First Nation groups in the country, the Innu have never signed a treaty nor in any other way, extinguished title to their territory.

In 1981, the Federal Government sanctioned the use of Innu land for low-level flight testing. It is projected that the number of flight of these high powered jets, which fly approximately 100 feet above ground at a speed of 900 km/hr, will increase from 7,800 per year in 1988 to 40,000 in 1992. Canada also offered to allow NATO to build a 800 million dollar Tactical Fighter Weapons Training Centre in Goose Bay, Labrador, which threatened to increase the number of flights multi-fold. Plans for the training centre were called off in May of 1989, but the current number of flights will continue.

Despite the fact that the rapid depletion of the caribou herds due to the low-level flight testing has been confirmed by Innu hunters, scientific researchers, and organizations such as "L'Association des Pourvoyeurs du Noveau, Quebec (commercial harvesters of Caribou), the Federal Government refuses to take any action to halt or even cut back the flight testing. To make matters worse, several Innu people have been placed under arrest for conducting peaceful blockades of the NATO runways in Goose Bay.

The Migratory Birds Convention Act and The Flett Case

Henry Flett, a member of The Pas Indian Band in Manitoba, which falls under Treaty 5, was charged in 1985 with hunting out of season under the Migratory Birds Convention Act 'MBCA'. Flett in turn challenged on the grounds that his hunting rights flowing from Treaty 5 and Section 35 of the Constitution override the MBCA.

In March of 1990, the Manitoba Court of Appeal ruled in favour of Flett, yet, despite this judgement, Provincial Natural Resources officials continue to lay charges and the Department of Justice officials continue to prosecute Treaty Indians for hunting migratory birds.

The North American Waterfowl Management Act states that the Indian hunt of migratory birds encompasses only some 5% of the total kill. The other 95% are killed by non-Indian sport hunters. Consequently, it is clear that the exercise by Treaty Indians of their hunting rights is in no way a threat to the viability of migratory bird populations in North America. Yet, First Nation hunters continue to bear the brunt of prosecutions.

First Nations find this international treaty to be a legalized form of harassment and discrimination. The issue at hand is simple: all prosecutions under the MCBA are initiated in Provincial Judges Courts; and, Provincial Judges are bound by the decisions of the Court of Queen's Bench. It is therefore a meaningless exercise to prosecute Treaty Indians because the charges, in all likelihood, will be dismissed by Provincial Judges. Nevertheless, Justice officials have indicated their intention to continue to prosecute.

E. PROTECTING THE ARCTIC ENVIRONMENT

Dene Nation Input into The Norman Wells Project

The Norman Wells Project in NWT which began in the 1970's is one of the largest oil pipeline projects in the world. From the government and industry's point of view, the project was a great success - no major environmental disasters, no work slowdowns, no acts of violence or political attempts to stop construction. But for the Dene, the history of the project, from start to finish, represents a gradual erosion of Dene rights to control or even have influence over control of development in their territory.

The Dene Nation originally opposed approval of the Norman Wells project, prior to a settlement of aboriginal rights and title. However, due to various outside pressures, Dene leaders reluctantly gave their conditional acceptance to the project with hopes of setting a precedence for a claims position on non-renewable resource development.

DIAND, the agency charged with responsibility for all environmental regulations in the north, was also a one-third owner of the oilfields in question, and therefore had a vested interest in seeing the project proceed as smoothly as possible.

From the point of view of the Dene, as people who use and depend on the resources of the land, the environmental protection measures required on the project were simply not strict enough to provide the level of environmental protection that the communities wanted. At first, no overall monitoring agency was established for the project. Instead it was done by existing government agencies, mostly DIAND and the National Energy Board, who rejected any Dene contribution.

After two years of fighting for government action on problems with the health of Mackenzie River fish downstream from Norman Wells. the Dene Nation was successful in getting the Department of Fisheries and Oceans to agree to initiate a joint study to try and determine what was causing the problems.

A sub-committee of Native organizations and communities, known as the Norman Wells Joint Environmental Working Group (NWPJEWG), was established. The Dene felt that the Group could have made a difference in the overall project impact of the Dene Nation had the funds and staff resources to make the group work. But, in the minds of the Dene the NWPJEWG, chaired by the Federal Coordinator's Office, became nothing more than a token attempt to address Dene concerns.

Several environmental concerns surfaced during the construction of the Project that the Dene Nation felt have not been adequately addressed by the monitoring regime. The Dene charged that the release of oil into the water had contributed to an overall reduction of water quality in the river. Exposed floating sections of pipeline were also frequently found in the river. They felt that impacts of the Project on renewable resource harvesting was not given full consideration. In addition, the Dene were sceptical about the adequacy of contingency plans for oil spills.

Conclusion

The examples cited in this paper are intended to illustrate that First Nations have deep rooted concerns and are directly impacted by all of the environmental issues identified in the Green Plan Framework. Furthermore, our unique world view translates into an equally valuable way of doing things. We believe that our world view must be combined with mainstream science and technology to assist in solving the very real and urgent environmental problems affecting our communities, the people of Canada and, indeed, the entire world.

Greg Young-Ing

Earth Memory

my beloved
beautiful
life-giving
sacred
curving
Earth

you are:

the oldest
Elder

the wisest
teacher

the ultimate
survivor

Creation warrior

remember
when the sharpest sensation felt
was a rumble
of charging buffalo hoofs
massaging your shoulder
or smashing buffalo heads
flying over cliffs
and poking your thigh

remember
in cherished time
when your back only knew
the soft caress
of moccasins
before hard heeled shoes
pounding
like workboots

remember
these mountains
could not imagine
the theft
of entire tree gardens
leaving raw aching skin
exposed
underneath scorching sun
like a whiteman's bald head

remember
before the massive weight
of smothering concrete
before scarring
with shovels
the pussing
of wells
and bleeding
in pipelines

remember
my ancestors

Duane Marchand

Tears From The Earth

ROM
F #
S #
R # #
A # #
E # #
T # #
H # #
u E # #
p # #
u E # #
p A #
u R T H
p
str
eam
a silver
brook trickles
tear-like from the
craggy face of a receding
glacier time has eroded valleys
ravines undergound caves and the stream
tumbles forward picking up speed silt poisons
from man fish gather and die great hunters eat
the numbers perish and pass into the earth the brook
moves on dragging effluent and chemicals from shoreline
mills mercury is the silver in the silver brook the
children play in their blood soon to burn in the
choking industrial air marine life lives with
the label toxic waste pinned to their
sightless eyes and stillborn babies
and the horrors of extinction
and they cry... upstream
a silver brook trickles
tear-like from the
craggy face of a
receding
glacier

(Song) 500 Years

You've had 500 years
to show us your better way
Is this your idea of good?
poverty and pain

CHORUS

> Why can't we make you see the light?
> We are red, we will not be white
> Why must push always come to shove?
> Why must we fight for what's already ours?

You took us from our homes,
our language, and our land
forget all that we've learned
not by choice but by demand

CHORUS

Mother Earth provides us well
take what you need and leave the rest
stop all your stealing and lies
Mother earth has nothing left

CHORUS

END

Jack Forbes

When Professors Die

How much time was left? A few seconds?

Only minutes, at the most. Maybe only a heartbeat and then it would all be over. In the utter darkness I kissed her lips, felt her body against mine. She was quiet, waiting.

I stroked her hair, squeezed her tightly, listening to the soft, hissing sound close by.

For some reason I smiled to myself. Here I was, thirty years old and yet I couldn't remember anything except what had occupied the last hour or so. Somehow my life had become compressed, even as the darkness now pressed in on me. It was compressed spatially, to this little washroom, and, temporarily, to these last few moments.

Was it the pain? Did I have to kill the memory of all of those I loved, in fact, of the death of everything? A healing insanity, compassionate amnesia? Is that what it was?

An hour earlier I had been attending a meeting upstairs, in the School of Education offices. I couldn't recall much, except that we were listening to the controversial theories of Doctor Chamberlain Stoddard, a professor who was trying to prove that Blacks and Indians had lower I.Q.s than whites and that our inferiority was permanent, genetically-based.

And yet, I could recall some of my comments. Of course, I had argued that Stoddard's White, Black and Indian populations were not genuine groups but were, in fact, simply arbitrary agglomerations of genetically, culturally, and socially distinct aggregates. But the thing that stuck in my mind now was what one Chicano colleague had said: "Doctor Stoddard, would there be more or less genocide and mass murder and torture in the world if we eliminated people with high I.Q. scores or low I.Q. scores...? What about El Salvador and Guatemala and Argentina and South Africa, Professor? Do we know the I.Q. scores of those who have unleased terror like a wild beast upon us?"

Stoddard chose to ignore all such soft arguments. Science will solve all of our problems. We must use quantitative science. Emotional considerations should be set aside. Cold, dispassionate science...

That phrase, "Science will solve all of our problems," ran through my head.

"God, how strange it is!" I muttered. Here I was in a different city from the one in which I lived. Fate, like a razor-sharp knife, had severed my life into two parts. Now there was only the before which I had cast aside and the after which was still sharp and clear.

My life began my present life when I accepted the inevitability of my impending death and I started to live with the rhythm of my death song.

My memory began retracing the events of my new life-the one which had commenced less than an hour before. I was sitting with other professors in the seminar room when a secretary outside started screaming. We all jumped up and rushed out to see what was wrong. People were already running through halls and offices with fear masking their faces.

"It just came over the intercom and on the radio we're about to be destroyed nuclear missiles have been fired bombers are in the air my children are still at school-- oh God!"

Sirens had started screaming. Everyone was running towards the stairways or trying to pack themselves into overloaded elevators.

I could feel the adrenalin surge through my body and I began to panic also. But then I caught myself. What was there to do? Death was certain. My home was far away. No way I could reach there. I couldn't do anything for anybody except those nearby.

I picked up a phone and tried to call my mother in a distant city. No use. The phones were all busy or out-of-order. Probably the phone employees had all abandoned their offices.

What to do? I thought back to the teachings of the elders, of Black Elk and Lame Deer, of Don Juan and the ancient poems of the Aztecs. The moments of death are precious. One must not panic. Whatever time I have left belongs now only to me. I must use it well.

I saw a familiar secretary leaning against a door frame, as if exhausted. She was a young brown woman I had admired before. "Arenda, what do we do now?" I said quietly. "Oh, man!" she replied, putting her arms out toward me. I took them and pulled her close.

"I can't do nothin," she sobbed. "My folks are too far away. I can't get to 'em in time. I just don't know what to do. Those goddamn son-of-a-bitches in the Pentagon...and the Kremlin too...They're killin' all of us."

"Yeah, I know. It looks like they're gonna kill off the whole white race and we just got caught in the middle.... They're all gonna be dead Arenda, just like us....Anyway, listen, I haven't got anybody either."

I hugged her tight. "Why don't we go someplace and be together. That would be better than just cryin and a lot better than killing. Besides, I've always wanted to tell you that you're a fantastic¬lookin woman."

"You crazy Indian! I always wondered how *you* could be a professor. You didn't have books on your mind all the time huh?"

We decided to go down to the basement of the building. Arenda said there were a lot of rooms down there.

Just as we were going into a big storage room underground I

spotted Professor Stoddard.

He was crouched against a wall, fear written all over his face. He was shaking and as I passed by I could smell the odor of human faeces. He couldn't control his organs and a pool of urine had collected where he was huddled.

I had never talked to the man individually before, mostly out of fear that I would lose my temper; but now some compulsion drew me toward him. Just then a Black graduate shouted, "Professor Stoddard? You've always argued that we non-whites are intellectually inferior. Okay, man what's the I.Q. of the bastards setting off these missiles? Is this the final genocide carried out by your superior Western Civilization?"

He looked at us in stark terror but he appeared to understand the question.

"Doctor Stoddard? I want to know something? Who dies easier? A man with a high I.Q. or a man with a low I.Q."

The one-time arrogant professor turned away to retch on the wall. I didn't feel sorry for him, however, because I knew that white men of his same mentality and hard cold insensitivity had planned the deaths of all of us.

"Professor? How do you qualify compassion? How do you quantify love? Can you measure greed on one of your tests?... Doctor I ask you again; are these members of the I.Q. super-race who have brought us to this?"

Arenda had been looking on in disbelief. But now she started laughing, rather hysterically, I thought, and then shouted at the trembling, heaving academic, "I always thought you were a big pile of shit, *Doctor* Stoddard. Now you can use your studies of all those I.Q.s to wipe up your own vomit with!"

The good professor was now gagging on his own bile and we left, but the grad student got off one parting shot: "Tell me professor, do high I.Q. or low I.Q. people suffer less from radioactive poisoning...or from radiation burns? Shall we see? Shall we get everybody's I.Q. score down here and then to a study after its all over? You can become famous...in Hell!"

Finally I said, "The Creator will judge your work doctor and that of all your colleagues from Moscow to Los Alamos!"

Most of the people in the basement were huddled against walls, with blank faces and staring eyes. Some were praying, some were quietly moaning, a few were shrieking. I took Arenda's hand and together, we began investigating all of the hallways, closets, laundry rooms, and so on. Finally we located a supply and wash room, where there were some gas-fired hot water heaters. We went in to wait, alone, away from the others.

"There's two things I want to do now. I want to pray for all living things and I want to be close to you. I want our deaths to be as beautiful as possible and...well, I want to die in touch with someone, because that's a prayer, too."

We both prayed for those that we loved, for the beautiful earth, for the trees and plants, for all living things. We were angry at what the U.S. government had done to us in the name of a defense which was really only mass murder. But we gradually cleansed ourselves of hate and bitterness, and reached a state of strange calmness.

I shut off the gas valves, turned off the lights, and, in total darkness, began holding her close. At that moment all hell broke loose. The warheads began hitting the area. The noise was deafening, beyond comprehension, and the building shook like an earthquake was underway. We could hear walls or floors and ceilings collapsing and glass shattering...and screams.

But we didn't surrender to terror. Driven by an elemental force, we desperately loved each other, seeking through the magic and power of love to give birth to a counterbalance to all of the evil unleashed by obstinate madmen.

And somehow we lived through that first attack. Our room remained intact. Still we knew that there was no escape from death, without food, without a permanent supply of clean air, and with no place to go even if we could have gotten out of our sanctuary.

And we did not want to seen the melted faces, the running eyes, the burned bodies, the severed limbs.

And so we lay there, naked, caressing each other and talking of love and of the next life, and of what we would say to our loved ones when we met them, and of the Indian prophecies.

We are all just a part of the Great Mystery. Now we are going to experience a transformation. We are shedding skins. But the Great Mystery, which is us, will go on.

Finally, in a period of rest, Arenda said, "I want to go now. I'm ready to die. I don't want to wait any longer. I can hear the fires getting closer."

I could also feel the increasing heat generated by fires somewhere outside of our room. I reached in the darkness for the gas jets and turned them all on.

As we lay together, there, in love, death crept up around us, hissing softly.

Irene Akiwenzie and Katerie Damm

A Little White Paddle and the Ice on the Bay (Oratory)

This is a true story. It was told to me by my grandmother, Irene Ahwenzie, who was told it by her father Charles Kegedonce Jones who was there. I will tell you the story in much the same way I heard it told many times as my family and friends sat drinking tea at my grandparents' table. That is the best way to hear the story, around a table full of people laughing, talking and drinking tea. This is also a good way to share a story and since my grandmother believed that stories are for sharing, not saving, I think she would be glad I am sharing the story with you here.

The events of this story took place at the Cape Croker reserve many years ago when my great-grandfather, Charles Kegedonce Jones was eight years old. He lived down in the village at the bay, at a place called Jones' Point. When you stand at the shore at Jones' Point, as you look out over the water you can see two bluffs, one on each side of the bay.

My great-grandfather Charles was eight years old at the time. It was late winter and the people were getting ready to go to the Sugar Camp to make maple sugar. In early March everything was ready. Everyone went - grammas, grampas, uncles, aunties, and children too. They took a big syrup pot with them to the Sugar Camp at the top of the bluff and they made baskets out of birch bark to catch the sap.

There were many maple trees, big hardy trees, at the Sugar Camp and so before long they had made all the sugar that they would need. Charles' brother, Peter Kededonce Jones was the Chief. He asked the people to take everything to the shore to be loaded into the canoes but he told some of the men to bury the big syrup pot at the camp so that they would not have to cart it back and forth every spring. Although everyone enjoyed being at the camp, food was running low and they knew it was time to go back home. With everyone helping the preparations were soon completed. The next morning they would leave by canoe.

That night a great northern blizzard blew in and all of the ice piled into the bay. It was very cold and by the fourth day of the storm everyone was cold and hungry. On that day Charles could not find his father in the camp. He went looking and found him outside the camp, whittling a little white paddle.

"Is it for me?" Charles asked.

"No," his father said. "This paddle will take us home."

How could it? Charles thought. It was so tiny.

"You stay here," his father said. "I have business to take care of."

With that he walked away. But being a curious eight year old boy Charles followed his father. He wanted to find out how a tiny paddle could take them all home when the bay was full of ice. The sun was settling. When his father stopped Charles hid and watched him. Great-great-grandfather Peter brushed the snow from a huge flat rock, put the paddle down, sprinkled it with tobacco and raised his hands towards the sky. Charles ran back to camp knowing that this was not for him to see. It was between his father and the Great Spirit.

When his father returned to camp he assembled everyone for a meeting.

"Now men," he said. "Load the canoes. Pack everything in solid and tight. We are going home tomorrow."

"But what about the ice? We can't leave," they said.

"When the first rays of sun come over Jones' Bluff we must go," he told them.

So, the next morning before light, everything was ready but the ice was still solidly packed in the bay. The people waited patiently. Then the sun began to rise and when the first rays came over Jones' Bluff, a crack, wide enough to paddle two canoes abreast, appeared in the ice.

"Hurry," Great-great-grandfather said. "We must be home before the last rays of the sun come over Jones' Bluff."

There was a great rush of activity as people began jumping into canoes and paddling furiously for home. Everywhere people were scurrying, men were shouting and water was flying from the paddles. The people paddled as quickly as they could, well aware of the ice on either side of them and of the rapidly rising sun. So, they paddled more quickly than they thought possible and soon they were home, pulling the canoes out of the water.

As the last canoes were pulled ashore, the last rays of the sun came over the bluff. Suddenly the crack in the ice came together and it remained so for three weeks.

The people gave thanks to the Great Spirit for saving them. They had kept their faith in the Great Spirit and it had been rewarded.

That is the story my great grandfather has given to us.

SPRING

Katerie Damm

An Old Woman in Spring

she stood by the fire burning on the hill above the river
watching the moon while stamping her feet into the ground
it was an early spring evening
the kind of sinking spring day
when the earth seeps into your skin if you let it
if you let it it starts with your toes
working without hurry without threat
like a melting of snow or a shedding of scales
later she walked to the water's edge
to listen to the wind
and saw the moon and water playing like children
and she went spinning and shouting along the shore
seeing her shadow sharing their game as if she were a child too
then she sat on a rock singing
closed her eyes remembering other nights in spring
and other children dancing on the earth
she was cold and stiff when her eyes opened again
an owl sat watching from the blackness
she saw his eyes shining like small moons
she watched him and listened afraid of what he might say
he turned away from her then
and disappeared without sound

Katerie Damm

What The Earth Might Say

there is no true silence
everything every bird and blade of grass
calls out its story as it must
and though you may see nothing
even the empty places are filled with meaning
respect too the spaces
inside them another language speaks
but to learn it you must listen
for tongues once stolen
now sing the wisdom of your saints
so listen like a forest
sometimes love and hate cry out
beyond the range of your ordinary hearing
so shrug off the coils that separate you from your brothers
put off the veil that covers your soul
take the scales from your eyes
see and hear like a true human

William Oandasan

My Old Times Ones

1

a valley ripe with acorns
and yellow poppies everywhere
as i stand here
dreaming of you

2

in chipped and tattered
weavings of a willow basket
the voice of an ancient age
dreaming of breath

3

in a chert arrowhead speckled with quartz
i have seen our grandfathers
along a stream east of the valley
lancing salmon and deer

4

swimming up the Eel
a spirit sings corn-
pound-the-old-way-draws-
the-milk-of-earth

5

from fresh currents of night air
above manzanitas near the cemetery
the words of ancient lips
turn in our blood again

6

a few traditions live
alongside a garden walk
in two large stones
now called mortar and pestle

7

long ago black bears
sang around our lodge fires
tonight they dance
alive through our dreams

Gunargie O'Sullivan

Envision The Invisible

I
(Before)

It was time to take my first step
into depths unknown
Dream thoughts enlightened
the fear I felt
My loss of breath amplified
the fears placed upon me
My soul cried out for healing ways
a different way
from that which surrounds me
I looked into the darkness
to envision the invisible

I stepped slowly
into the power
of the Mother Land
where I would be who I am
the earth child
mother, daughter, sister
and friend

There I saw a limy green circle encircled by red, the colour of the hosts and the blood of our People. It was not a dream. It was a circle of many meanings. Greatness greeted me, as I looked upon it looking at me. I felt relief from my fear. I was comforted by its presence

"Are you scared?"
"No, I'm not scared at all."
"Have your coffee, finish it off.
Come to our learning lodge
and you shall receive what I will give."

The last one in, I sat on a buffalo hide. Then I listened for guidance, explanations and prayer.

II
(During)

Sure as sun set
I became a part of Buffalo Women
giving thanks to some other
than god himself

Women of power
Power of women
Words of power
Power of words

Our women undressed
beneath starlite beauty
We placed cotton sheets
around our uncleansed souls
One after the other
offering tobacco to the women of power
the teacher of the lodge
each asking Grandfathers
to listen to our prayers

One by one, we gave fire tobacco from our left hands. With the right hand, we left an offering to the rock placed on the East side of the sacred fire. This rock is called "Young Boy", named after the one who had this way brought back to the people.

Through the door on hands and knees, careful not to cross cedar trail, I sat to the North with my prayers waiting and awakening. Grandfathers came from all directions. North, South, East, West.

Songs, rattles, language,
and words of wants and needs
of others for others
breathing the breath of ancestors
kissing Earth Mother
unspoken words heard
and answered

III
(After)

No magic
but true beauty
in blackness
I witnessed
inward and outward
every way I turned
I felt beauty and blackness

"Earth Power, where have I been? I have stayed away from you for so long? Surely the others can see too. I told you Grandfather and you received. And now I believe."

All my relations
come now
stop the other man
from another land
Let them see
their own darkness
from within

"Don't let what has been done be done again. It's been too long since I have spent time with our kind of power."

"You grandfather, you have brought me back to my own reality. You let me feel, see, and be one with you. When will you touch the others who are drifting to enlighten them with your higher power? Do I ask too much, or is it you asking through me? I know you know what I didn't say and that has always been a comfort to me."

Now I will communicate with you
being with you again and again
hoping through prayer
for you to spread
across this white trodden land
through buried valleys
across hungry plains
over sagging mountains
from woman to man
black or white
yellow and red

Let all of the colours
of this precious land
come back
shining stars
of Earth beauty
reflected
on dream power
up in the fearless sky

Peter A. Ettagiak

My First Hunting Trip (Oratory)

The story I'm going to tell you happened in 1970, but to me it is like yesterday. It was May, the month of my 8th birthday. At that time my family was living across the Mackenzie Delta.

One day, close to breakup time, many hunters were going out for seals. We were all on the ice when my grandfather Sam, my uncle William, my little brother Samuel, and I floated away on the ice. All we had with us were our dogs and our qamutik (sled).

The wind was blowing from the south. We could not get back any more, so we started to walk on the ice. For 14 days we walked, looking around for thicker, safer ice. Some days it was warm, some days cold. We became very thirsty. We couldn't eat snow; it would have made us even thirstier.

One day Uncle William shot a walrus on top of the ice. He opened it up and cleaned it out. Then he put snow into it and it melted fast because the walrus was still warm. That day we drank a lot of water.

We put pieces of the walrus meat on the qamutik and took pieces from the walrus to sleep on. At night we pulled up big blocks of ice from the ocean and put them together for shelter or, if we had enough snow, we built an igloo.

Every night my little brother Samuel slept inside Uncle William's parka, keeping warm from his body. During the daytime we kept on walking.

Finally, the wind changed and we got close to a small island that is called Tuktoyaktuk, not far from Inuvik. The ice was very thin, and we all kept running fast for fear it would break under our feet. We barely made it to the island when the ice disappeared.

One day a man came so close to the island with his kayak that we could even see him smoking his pipe. Sam made the dogs bark loud, but the man didn't hear them. When he went home, his wife told him she had heard dogs and yelling on the island, but the man said, "You didn't hear anything but yourself."

My grandfather Sam made a flag by putting his parka on the harpoon, but nobody saw it. Sam was a good man, always trying to help others. He knew the weather like nobody else did.

For nearly two weeks we waited. We had hardly any food left when, finally, a big wind came from the north and brought ice all around the island. Sam and Uncle William walked back to the island. They had been gone for more than a month.

When we arrived at our home, my little brother was riding on the qamutik. He was so happy, he just ran into the igloo in his little caribou parka. Everybody had thought he was dead. Uncle William just started yelling and crying. I was happy to be home; I thought, "Now we are not going to die any more."

That night we all sat around the warm fire, remembering our adventure. Uncle William looked at me and smiled proudly. "You are a brave, tough little Eskimo like me," he said.

Lee Maracle

Scarlet Requiem

From the window scarlet leaves danced. The air outside crunched cold against the pane inside. The coolness drifted over the top of the vinyl cover on the back of the home-made bench couch he kneeled on. He could feel it. It pricked his nose whenever he pressed it up between the wooden bars that separated the panes of glass. His warm breath against the cool air was vaporous. It clouded his view. It misted the dancing leaves. He could still hear them though, slipping, sliding, and whistling their way through their last song before winter put them all to rest on the earth below. No one in the room paid any attention to the leaves. He turned to look in the direction of the murmuring voices. Through a large doorway he could see his aunts leaning forward intently and whispering. The men in the room didn't seem to have anything to do with the kitchen table conversation. Most of then hovered about the old Mclary stove or leaned against a doorway or wall. Some of them smoked quietly. One of them sat in a corner of the room Paulie was in. His elbows rested on his knees while his eyes let go a steady stream of tears but he made no sound. Paulie couldn't figure out why neither the dying leaves nor he called anyone to attention. He wasn't sure why this moment was eerie, maybe scary, but he was sure it was. A single leaf cut loose from the herd above and floated, helter skelter, to the pane of glass. It hit the pane at his eye level. It made him start. He jumped away from the window. Like the people in the room, its movement was erratic and urgent looking.

Bits and pieces of words floated around him. They followed the movement of more leaves. These words didn't seem to have much to do with him. Every now and then some tearful woman picked him up, held him, shed a few tears, then deposited him back at the window pane. He accepted these hugs without response, then he resumed his death watch over the sugar maple in the yard. The noise today was unusual, uncomfortable. Maybe it wasn't loud enough. He didn't really know what was wrong with the noise. But it was wrong. Besides, there were too many people in the room.

Death's usual reverence was uncomfortable for these women who looked forward to life. The death of Paulie's mom didn't inspire reverence. She was too young. He heard his one aunt whisper that it was obscene for her to leave so soon. Fearful resignation settled in on the faces of the women who needed death's reverence to feel comfortable, hopeful. The murmurs were steady, the sounds all muffled, the meaning unclear. He turned to look at the moving figures, all large, all just a little edgy. Nothing was smooth. Everyone spoke in soft low tones, but their bodies couldn't lie. They didn't look soft, jerking about stiffly as they were, and weeping every time they caught sight of him.

The stiffness, the tears, the unsuccessful fight for reverence scared him. He returned to the view outside. His hands pressed against the sill's edge with grim determination. His knuckles whitened slightly under the tan brown of his fingers. He had no name for this change in color. No name for the murmuring bustle behind him. No name for the sound of wind through the sugar maple or the whisper of leaf after leaf as the wind tore them from the tree. The tree mothered these leaves; he could feel this motherhood and he tried to wonder why she cast them off in the cold wind, but no words took shape in his mind - just feelings.

Feelings of dread. Feelings of cold. Violent feelings grew inside Paulie as the hustle and bustle of people, who failed to find reverence, intensified and they grew stiffer and stiffer with the effort. Sad feelings mingled with cold air and the foggy vapor of his breath clouded the riot of sugar maple's colors. He had no name for the colors. The absence of names for the colors deepened his sadness. He had no idea why.

One of the men, his daddy, sat tense in his chair. He said nothing. He never looked at Paulie. Every now and then, one of the other men would touch his shoulder, but the man never moved. All day he sat and stared as he drank cup after cup of coffee. The sound of him sipping coffee seemed to intensify his morose silence.

There was a shift in tension in the room behind him. It made him start and want to guard his back. The voices became crisper, more definitive. Each woman took turns laying out the situation as she saw it. His name came up every now and then. He cringed at the mention of his name in the context of unfamiliar language and unknown decision-making. The old woman in the corner changed his name. He didn't recognize this new name. He thought they stopped talking about him, so he resumed his own death watch over autumn. A wet rag suddenly landed on him from his right side. He wasn't ready for it. It scraped at his face. He twisted, a hand clutched the top of his head and held him still. No sense struggling; the hand was too big, too determined.

"Hold still now," and she cleaned the tears and mucus from his face. The edge in her voice was new. A ball of hot sound swam up from his chest to his face. He was about to let it go.

"Don't cry, now," she cajoled softly, almost sweetly, and he stopped, confused. "Don't cry now?" These words were new; Mommy never said them. A dark whirl set itself in motion in his mind. A whirl of movement, images of some other time he couldn't define. No names for days, nights, weeks - just a generic sense of before. Before it was o.k. to cry. Before, there weren't all these people here, just Mommy, Daddy, and Paulie. Paulie, the name glided about, shrank, grew small and distant.

Panic. He could feel it. It was a memory so close to now. Mommy, something happened to Mommy and in the whirl of images a moment was held, smokey-looking and unclear, but very still. In this moment, Mommy was near the door, trying to leave. She didn't look quite right. She leaned against it, slid down the length of its frame, then collapsed. Above her Paulie could see a spider drop toward her. It hung ominously on a single silken thread. She looked so big and so small at the same time. Slowly the spider drifted toward her. It threatened to land on her face. He turned away and caught sight of the view behind him of leaves falling helplessly to the ground. He panicked. Screams came from somewhere inside of him so foreign sounding and full of terror that he wasn't sure who it was that screamed. He ran toward her and grabbed her dress. A hand moved to get him out of the way. The hand jerked at the little boy who could still hear the scream. Another pair of hands pried the boy's fingers loose and the big hand tossed him aside. The images in the room grew fuzzy. Paulie could see a little boy crouched in the corner, mouth open and no sound coming out but he was too unfamiliar with his own face to know it was him. At the recollection of this memory his hand clutched the sill. He tried to help his mind hold onto the memory. It felt important to hold the memory still, to look at it, but it slipped far away in the dark tunnel from where it came.

A decision was made, a decision he had no name for. The feeling of its finality set in. The women rose and began removing things from the shelf. Paulie's hand went up. He reached in the direction of the women who took Mommy's things and put them in boxes. No one paid attention to his hand. What had they decided? The nameless presence of their decision and their current actions overwhelmed him. The panic rose, grew intense. It rested in the center of the finality which took up all the space but for the small piece of his panic. The finality gained weight. It pressed up against the small boy, pushed him closer to the wall. He could hardly hold his head up. His eyes looked at the floor. He pushed back on the finality. His panic subsided. Push back. It settled the insides to push back.

"Paulie. Get away from that window," and the young woman reached for him. He didn't move. Push back. Hold the sill. Watch the leaves. Let the room have its movement, its scary rhythym, its finality. Paulie will stay put. She couldn't move him by herself. Soon another set of hands helped to loosen his grip and the other swung him upward. He froze. "You're not my mom." It came out rich with threat, full of push back, but the room only laughed its venom. The body of the boy was too small to carry out the threat that laced his voice. They knew it and found his words amusing. He knew it too, but it felt good to say it. She held him up, smiled. Paulie didn't smile back. He glared, just for a moment, then pushed that down inside. It whirled delicately inside - a tiny leaf of red emotion he cast downward to some place deep within his body. It whistled a high pitched scream only Paulie heard as it floated and landed with a quiet whisper somewhere deep inside. She tossed him gently up and down. His eyebrows rose, almost skeptically so; his eyes grew dark, full of threat; it scared the woman, and she stopped. He was aware he had scared her. He made her put him down with just a look - a cold, intense look. He felt power surge inside as he ended his aunt's intrusion this simply.

Paulie tasted this moment of power. He grabbed hold of it hard. He practiced all day until dark dropped over him. He would have forgotten about it, but the next day bloomed the same as the one before...the window, the sugar maple tossing off her leaves, the bustle, the stiff bodies and their incongruously reverent voices, and, eventually, the finality of another decision made, confusing him again and then panic followed. The pushing back rose of its own accord. It came without the need for memory to call it back to life. It came over and over, each time the moment of decision brought the feeling of finality to the room. The colder Paulie's push the more effect it had on the women around him and the more powerful he felt. His cold glare always ended any unwanted intrusion on his person. It changed the way people spoke to him. Sometimes it even altered the way they moved around the room. At first, however, it didn't seem to permanently discourage them. They all took turns trying to solicit some sort of happy response from him. Each by turns were unnerved by the intensity of his cold glare and, finally, they all gave up.

By the third day he became familiar with the sound of the words "Aunt" and "Uncle." He already knew his gramma's and grampa's names. Other words came up that took on familiarity with the repetition of them. "Funeral"..."ceremony"..."after the funeral"..."after the ceremony." Finally, his mommy returned. He giggled and laughed triumphantly when they wheeled her in on the same bed that had taken her away. He knew she would be back. She was sleeping. He made a dash for her. He leaped straight from the bench and landed on the wheeled bed. His hands grabbed her dress and he screamed, "Wake up, Mommy!" Voices barked, hands went out and he rose in the air again.

"Get away from there," and he felt panic again. His scream died in his throat; it moved outside to where the leaves hurled themselves at the earth. What have they done to Mommy? His tongue moved about in his head, searching for the shape of the words. He knew these words, "What have they done to Mommy", but his tongue was unfamiliar with the shape it would have to make to form the words. He looked at the gurney, mouth open, eyes wide and let the panic seize him. His skin grew tight. His muscles pressed against his bones inside. The skin got tighter still. His lungs let go all their air. Everything was so tight, no air wanted to go back inside. His shoulders hunkered down and his hands formed fists. A knot formed in his gut.

He turned his head one last time to look at his mom. she lay so completely still. She was so still, she looked small, frail, despite her weight. The hands carried him past lines of people - aunts, uncles, older cousins. They reached for his cheek, looked shyly sympathetic at him. Underneath the sympathy, there lay the tightened musculature of faces who struggled for some form of nameless control. Paulie did not believe in the nameless surface of sympathy. He saw the tightness behind the faces. He believed the tightness. He felt it inside himself. Tightness is cold, stiff, like the old sugar maple dropping her leaves all over the place.

One by one, the people all left the house. The man with the huge hands went with the gurney. Paulie stopped his own breath as he watched his daddy take his mommy away. This phantom who came home every week-end and disappeared for most of the time was almost unknown to Paulie. Paulie didn't want his dad to take his mommy away. He couldn't find the words to object and they left.

Paulie had to stay. Funerals were not for babies. He lay on the couch, eyes vacant; he stared at the ceiling for a long time, while the young aunt who volunteered to stay behind with him read stories. She was well-meaning. She wanted to take his mind off the morbidity of his mother's funeral. From the couch, Paulie could still see out the window. Below the drone of his aunt's voice, he thought he could hear the sugar maple scream at the leaves, "Get away from there...get away from there...get away..." The sad sound of it whirled about and invaded him in some far away place he was unfamiliar with. It was too far away to make him cry.

He lay so still his aunt worried. She chucked his chin and tried to get some sort of response from him to no avail. He lay there as still as his mom had. It unnerved her. She began to read too fast; her voice got squeaky and went up a pitch higher than usual. She argued this fear into a perverse attachment of blame to Paulie. "Paulie's stubborn. He's spoiled." This helped her voice to finally lose its fear. The others had said something like this earlier whenever he glared at them, so she saw nothing wrong with her line of reasoning. She didn't recover her empathy for Paulie. The fear gone, her tone took on the finality Paulie now loathed.

The story lost all joy for Paulie. A hazy image of a woman, book in hand, rose above the sound of the woman's voice. There were smiles all over her, even her hands seemed to smile as she reached for Paulie. Her image tried to rise above the picture of screaming scarlet leaves. The image of Mommy fought for a while with the picture of falling leaves. He could see her mouth move. Her words failed to erase the sound of the leaves who pleaded for their lives. He tried to bury the sound of screaming leaves so he could hear his mommy. The screaming would not go away. Mommy's soft voice could not drown the screams and, finally, the image of her lost the fight and the screaming leaves seemed to weep. A lone tear hid behind Paulie's eyes. It tried to escape but failed. For a brief moment Paulie felt sorry for the leaves. His hand went up in the air as though to reach out and comfort them. They were too far away. His hand hung suspended for a second, then fell helplessly to his side. He tried to remember the leaves, the woman, and the sound of her, to hold the images still, but they slipped away.

In the days and weeks that followed people disappeared except for the occasional visit by one or two of them at a time.

Paulie didn't care much for the women who came unless they brought other children with them. They tended to behave as though he were each one of their personal toys. Gramma used these moments to complain about him, called him a handful, and the aunt who was visiting always supported her by bawling Paulie out. Big large fingers were shaken at him for things he couldn't remember doing. During these times, Paulie learned to be inconspicuous. As an aunt arrived he retreated to some corner and busied himself at nothing.

The uncles were easier to take. They accepted his invisibility more readily then did his aunts. Gramma's small complaints were met only by grunts from the men. They never interfered with his upbringing in the same way his aunts did. Wasn't any of their business. No one ever talked about Mommy - not our way, they said. By the time Paulie found the words to ask about his mom, he no longer wanted to know the answer.

Mostly, the house was empty. It felt lonely. There was a deep sadness all about the house. It filled every room. He stopped looking out the window so much. It didn't seem to help. The feeling of sadness grew almost comfortable compared to the wasted hope that lay in searching the window for something he could no longer define.

Daddy came by once in a while in the beginning. He had grown morose and Paulie came to dread his arrival. At the same time, he hoped for an end to his dad's moroseness. He behaved better when his dad came. Maybe this could encourage Dad to be happier. It didn't and slowly Paulie gave up.

He began to forget Mommy. The images grew hazier, less frequent and within weeks they all died. He stopped trying to drag them up. They were too vague and it tired him to do it. Instead he moved about the house of his gramma and searched for familiarity in the lines of his new home. Eventually, the walls took on ordinariness. The rooms became old friends. The sadness and the loneliness became a familiar ambience Paulie identified with. The different smells gramma made when she cooked grew welcome. Fed, he felt some comfort, but most of the time only cold curiousity governed his heart.

Earth grew white. He stared out the window and wistfully watched its whitening. He loved the whitening of each leafless branch. Leafless, the trees lost their scream and the white was so softly melancholy like himself that it was almost a comfort. He watched for something else too. He couldn't quite remember what it was he looked for...maybe Daddy...maybe some unnameable feeling.

Winter perished. Spring came and went, then summer took its turn. He matured some. He grew old enough to resent not being being allowed to go outside on his own, but he accepted his confinement as part of his general condition of estrangement and sadness.

Daddy doesn't live here. He came to this realization some time after hot summer days dwindled into cool mornings. The leaves outside began to orchestrate their own death requiem. His visits grew rarer with the intensification of reds over paling green.

Paulie couldn't remember the precise moment he saw it coming. Days merged into other days, memories layered themselves one on top of the other in some crazy fashion like leaves piled one upon the other, suffocating what lay beneath. Then, suddenly, it became clear Daddy wasn't coming back. For some reason Paulie took to wishing for his return. There was a reason beyond his daddy that Paulie could not remember. The moment it was clear he wasn't coming back, Paulie renewed his vigil at the window and stared at it. He stared out the window a lot. He waited for his dad. His dad was somehow connected to memories he couldn't bring up. He couldn't figure out why but he desperately wanted him to come back. He felt the desperation. Inside his mind he whispered "Daddy" with huge intensity as though to will his return. It didn't seem to matter how often he called him or how hard. Daddy never came back at all. Deep shame at his failure to recall his father paralyzed him for a long time. He became listless, withdrew into the world of immediate reality around him, and buried the world of whirling motions inside far from the compelling moments of the here and now. Finally, the words took shape. He had to wait a long time before their intensity subsided enough for him to dare ask his gramma.

"Gramma, Daddy doesn't live here no more?" he asked one day at breakfast. His voice remained nonchalant as he waited for the answer. He pushed hard at the sound of desperation which threatened to come back up. He pushed it back to where it now lived permanently wrapped up in a tiny scream far away from his mouth.

"No," she harumphed. "Now eat your breakfast." Paulie ate in dreadful silence..... Outside the leaves began anew their terrible ceremony. The wind blew and the sugar maple shook all her children from her trunk and just left them there on the ground to blow about mercilessly in the wind. Inside Paulie stared apathetically at the toast while he ate. He gave a cursory glance out the window at the sugar maple shaking off her leaves, then returned to his toast. He didn't remember that once he had felt so sorry for them all.

Jean Wasegijig

Horses In The Night

I heard the sound of hooves,
Late at night, near my village
Far away thunder sounds,
Getting closer.

The wild horses,
No one could catch or tame,
Living to roam.

Someone grabbed my small hand,
And over a rotted fence,
We jumped and towards a house
We ran, my feet now dragging.

The rumbling sound,
The rising dust,
The weathered refuge,
Under an array of stars.

In the old house, sat an old woman,
Rocking, knitting, talking,
Telling us a story of spirits
That walk in the night.
A shiver passed through me,
I wondered if that was one of them.

I heard the sound of hooves,
Fade away into the night,
Leaving only the sound of crickets,
And the old woman telling stories.

Jean Wasegijig

Children of the Earth

We've been here for a very long time,
Our children have been here longer,
So they tell me.

And what am I, but an old woman,
With stars for my eyes,
Shadows in moonlight cross my face.

My cape is black sometimes,
An ebony sheen, like my hair,
Falling, like wild whiskers,
To the whim of the southern wind.

My other cape is white,
A fusion of ivory and silver,
It covers everything.

I shiver in the cold, cover with the cape,
The white one that sparkles, shimmers,
Lights reflect from each woven strand.

I see between the flecks in my eyes,
In each tiny glitter, so small,
A reflection barely seen.

Throughout the day and into the night,
I hear a sound, getting louder, clearer,
A whistling, whirring sound.

It passes all of a sudden,
Sounds of whirlwinds,
Rushes by with a hush of a sigh,
Lifting my cape.

I don the cape of ebony,
The other falls aside,
Leaving a trail of crystal shadows.

Coloured rays,
Of jade, lapis and amethyst,
Cast a beam on my gnarled feet.

And what am I, but an old woman,
With stars for my eyes.

Chuck Rush

Breakin' Beads

The Whale People told
the Salmon Clan to take a message
to the people of the Turtle-Shell
A warning to spell in the stars a new-age

With heed the Raven was harkened and
labeled the task to the Owl Clan
sages gathered around to know where they
stand
this is the story the Cricket People wage

Each night reminded the forest world of what happened
when the Cougar Tribe and Wolf
camp met the Eagle Clan
where fraught a
scout on horse back with what the meanings wove....

The meanings of the sounds coming
from each councils' throats
meanings
conveyed to communicate
inflections exasperations
meanings of what the animal-peoples meant
each time they went and what exactly they said

The arrows to freedom will land
and years from now
families frayed and land lost will all return
but when the animals told the people
long ago the arrows landed and the quills
quivered
and now the Cricket people
have a new song - to learn.

Michael Paul-Martin

user-not-so-friendly

we're squareheads
Archie Bunker's
Humptee Dumptee
meathead mechanic
monkeys near far
En'owkin wall in
the Romper Room

on fullmoon days
we like to steal
assigned scrolls
chew them up at
no man's land
no woman's land
excuse says "moi"

don't like smokes
but coffee breaks
our lines become
crooks & warriors
even Mohawk hair
Crees & Micmacs
& Oka army tanks

we are programmed
to raise flags
for Ira Hayes
run through Inuit
syllabics rarest
Japenese writing
& h-bomb scribes

Alice Lee

Woman With No Face

Old Mother has spread her blanket of stars over all. My eyes are heavy with dreams as I sit beside Kookum. As I doze off, sitting beside my grandmother, I dream a quilt of blueberries wrapped around me. In my dream I nibble a corner of the quilt. I love the taste of blueberries.

Kookum shakes the dreams from my eyes. "The campfire is going out. Firedancer is ending his dance. Tomorrow we will pack up camp and return home. I will need your help to make pies and jams with the berries we've picked. Starlet, you must go to the river and bring water for morning."

I turn and look into my grandmother's face and know she sees the fear in my eyes but Kookum turns to the campfire in silence. "Please come with me", I plead silently. "It's dark. I don't know this dark. I wish I were back in the city with my mom. It's never this dark in the city."

I walk carefully toward the river. The path which is my friend in the day has become a stranger. My new running shoes shine white in the night. Kookum gave them to me. When I was smaller she used to make me beaded moccasins but now she says her hands are getting too old to sew and bead.

Many night sounds are loud in my ears. Fear begins a song in my throat. Fear's voice jumps from my throat and sings in my head. The voice becomes one with the darkness.

River is still while dreaming. As I lower my jug, my face becomes part of River's dream, singing now with fear on reflection under. River is still once more.

Another face climbs slowly up from River's depths. Tangled brown weed hair falls over this face. Pieces of garbage are caught in the tangles. My heart is still as River stirs in sleep and washes the hair away from the face. A woman with no face looks back at me.

The dark smell of death is strong in my nostrils. An evil smell. Fear beats in my heart as I drop my jug and turn to run. The earthen jug lies empty, forgotten. Behind me, it is as though an open throat reaches out to eat my flesh. I'm chased by the shadow of Fear's song as I run back to my grandmother.

My breathing is fast and loud as I run close to Kookum. She sits as still as the fire laying on the earth bed at her feet. "I saw a woman with no face!" I point to the river.

Kookum reaches out and holds me close to her. "The earth is a gift. Gifts must not be wasted. There were those people who held sacred all that was of the earth. There was respect for all things living and dead. Peoples' ways have changed. The earth is hurting. Her body is scarred and bruised. This woman with no face has shown herself to you. She is the injured spirit of the earth. We have to know that to hurt the earth is to hurt ourselves."

"I've become an old one and will soon die. I'll return to the earth and comfort her with my bones. Starlet, it's your birthright to hold sacred all that is of the earth. This woman with no face is of the earth. I'm going to give you a song in your mother's tongue. In our language. This is a holy song, a healing song. You must share it with others so that they too can know how to save the earth."

Kookum begins to sing. I listen to her voice. I know somehow that they are cries and chants of another time. The voice of a people. I listen so that I will know the words. I listen so that I too will sing for others to listen.

Joseph Dandurand

Swimming in the Cannon River

sleepy

eyes heavy

forgot to keep
my balance

fell into
the unforgiving
river

panic

followed by
release

slept
till they
pulled me
out

visions
of ghosts
and demons
never came

found
myself
swimming
with the
fish
i was to
catch

Warrior

his red face
long black hair
earrings—red beads

gentle sun—yellow

earth—green in places
and yet
blue
where water should be

a cross stands tall
its markings known
only to those who
put it there

trees — stand
a forest once
now it's cut down
to empty space

protest signs
awake us
and yet
where did the wood
come from

warrior
his face
becomes
not
red

Geraldine Manossa

Weeds

I dig. I uproot weeds, annoying clumps of green huddle soil. "This has not been done in months." I breathe barely above a whisper. My hands continue to grasp wispy grass. Clenched fists tug and pull. Clenched fists tug and pull.

teeth clenched
I swallow my tears
teeth clenched
I swallow my tears

"Why in the hell do weeds grow here?" I repeat with blame. The cross covers only patches of white paint, disrupts my words. I have more work to do.

The air is grey, and continues to intertwine with charcoal clouds which constantly transform. My eyes freely explore sky and search for a recognizable shape or pattern to show existence. "Yah, yah....I'll get to the paint," I mutter to my body. I leave the spot on Mother Earth which embraces my brother. I have work to do.

Confronted, a barbed wire fence teases me. I steady myself on a pole and I stretch wire to crawl through. Once safe and balanced, I turn around and face the grave. I nod in a subjective manner. "Go-ya, I am so easily distracted." One peek to the sky and no movement occurs. Colour is silent. Clouds I guess are done playing. I have work to do.

I walk along grass flat from many trips made to the graveyard. I know my auntie makes many trips for my brother, for her two sons. Her two sons lay wrapped in the same earth blanket my brother wears. I know every time her feet cross this yellow growth, her hands are equipped with a hoe. I continue to back-track the disaster that stole her two sons. The worn trail shows me my aunt's grief; her lonesomeness, the day she stopped being a mother, the day the water world overwhelmed her two babies and carried them under the dark side of a wave.

My aunt's front door conceals itself from endless poplar ash trees. A large part of the other half of land she lives on is settled with stone people, constantly being bathed every time water from the lake washes upon shore.

"Wesla," Auntie rushes toward me. I automatically think of Mom. Her eyes, like Mom's brown eyes, are stars encouraging me to dance to a song of beauty for all people young and old. Auntie sends warmth through her hugs. My chest is open to all creatures from the winged ones to the four-legged. My pride offers affection. There are no cement sidewalks here to limit your path, or skyscrapers to act superior and minimize your sight. I breathe freedom.

"You came alone?" She asks and sends calmness through her words, already knowing the answer.

"Yahh...alone, Mom stayed in the city." My eyes drag downward, following my words.

Aunt Clara does not need to hear the usual shit story of Mom being real busy. She has work to do, so I don't bother. She grabs my hand and leads me into the house. My fingernails, packed with dirt, catch her eyes. She immediately focuses to the graveyard. In a continuous nod she knows, "You were over there....ah."

Her motion halts; her chin is frozen pointing at the graveyard. For a moment memories flood and time is forgotten. The graveyard holds silence and as we continue to re-live the soft precious moments, she squeezes my hand. We have each other and a feeling of strength guides us into the present. We enter her home. She abandons me and disappears into her bedroom, the only other room in the home beside the kitchen and the living room. The power that led our thoughts to the present disappears with the freeing of our joined hands. I begin to remember.

Her home has the safe smell of moose hides
My ears listen to the walls
they are laughing
Go-ya and I both played here
fought a lot too
once
we both became lost
in our wrestling play
his head hits hard against wall
he quits the game
he says I am mean
My ears listen to the walls
they still cry

Auntie appears from her dimly lit bedroom. Bright colours of red, orange, and yellow are woven together, forming a bedroom door. They leave trails of welcome as she pushes aside the blanket. She smiles pleasingly and hands me a photograph.

She teases, "Here, give this to your boyfriend." The picture is of me in the water. I am naked. My open-mouth smile in the photo laughs love. I don't ever remember having an attitude about swimming nude. We kids just did. My eyes focus on the young girl. Her back faces waves readily, washes against her body.

Her body has no resistance.

Her body is a wave

"Yah, but Auntie, if I show this picture to him, he might get some ideas." I raise my eyebrows and tease with the same innocence as the light captured in the photo. We both laugh. I explode into a chuckle largely because of my own lack of confidence now to be able to swim without the restrictions of a bathing suit.

At night my uncle plays fiddle
Go-ya's body races with the rhythm
his legs carry the beat
to the Red River jig
in kitchen
brothers, cousins, sisters
dancing Metis magic
electrified and kept ignited
by wood burning stove

"You should wash up," my aunt offers. I wake from the music. She pours some hot water into the basin.

"Do you need a shovel?" she asks. I carve my nails into the soap bar.

"No, the weeds are small." The water already murky. "There are just a lot of them, that's all," I add, and continue to scrub.

My uncle's words rattle around in my thoughts. "Louis Riel, the hero." Auntie Clara adds more hot water from the kettle. In grade eleven Social Studies class my teacher taught me all I needed to know about Louis Riel. It was not difficult. He was a madman, a rebel, obviously crazy, and deserved to hang. I didn't even have a chance to fail that unit. They kicked me out. Something to do with my manner of speaking vented from only an insignificant source. Cree/Metis culture was to blame, and not the racism from the teacher where truth froze, passion died and parts of my history became undeveloped. My voice cannot evolve.

My uncle fiddled songs
chords expressed from heart
of a man
to a man
who worked for
Metis nation

"This one's for Louis," Uncle would holler, adding to memories of the aged wood within the echo of the walls. I wish he could have escaped or dug his way out but it was treason from the Canadian government, killing and digging away at Riel's spirit. The water in the basin is filthy. My hands are clean, except, for the stubborn soil filling the network of the lines on my palms. I empty the basin of water outside Aunt Clara's home. Splat against the grave.

I grab a shovel. My body desperately races toward the grave. With no control tears empty from my eyes.

"You assholes," looking up to the sky. My voice shakes. Clumsily it carries. "All you people do is shit on other people, and wipe yourselves clean, while others suffer form what they are limited from." Memories of Go-ya's funeral whirl around in my mind. I try to steady the confusion. I dig my feet into the earth.

His grave lowered into mud
rain poured
it wet the dirt
packed into my palm
to be returned to earth
as part of his blanket of soil

I do not know who was listening, but the cry from those words is sent to all the white people who hollowed out and turned over our soil of inner riches. I have more work to do.

A soil so fertile
to accept and bloom seeds
planted with our own hands
clear of weeds
gently picked.

Monique Mojica

A Fast Growing Mold Bitter As Shame

"It is the shaman's connection to the spirit world that Indian women writers reflect most strongly in our poetry and fiction. If there is any Indian woman's tradition that inform our work, it is the spiritual understanding of womanhood as an expression of spirit. That understanding is formed on the recognition that everything is alive, that the spirit people are part of our daily world, that all life lives in harmony and kinship with and to all other life, and that sickness of all kinds and of all orders comes about because of our resistance to surrendering to the complexity and multidimensionality of existence. So we acknowledge that the violation of the Mothers' and Grandmothers' laws of kinship, respect, balance, and harmony brings about social, planetary, and personal illness and that healing is a matter of restoring the balance within ourselves and our communities. To this restoration of balance, of health, and wellness (wealth) we contribute our energies. For we are engaged in the work of reclaiming our minds, our gods and our traditions; the sacred hoop cannot be restored unless and until its sacred center is recognized."
- Paula Gunn Allen - "The Sacred Hoop" - Beacon Press, 1986

SCENE 1

(Bedroom area; 2 figures silhouetted as a dark form. They are supported against each other and are upright, but each is asleep and does not hear the other's voice. Their voices come from the crack between the dreamworld and the waking world.)

WOMAN The fine hairs, the cilia, seductive tendrils as permeable as smoke, soft as mist, insidious as fog that obscures the path, mutes the footfall.

MAN Invading all boundaries, searching, probing, creeping like a fast-growing mold. It lays its sucking tentacles across my mouth and nose gulping, swallowing my breath, devouring all light.

WOMAN I don't know how it got in here! My door was locked and bolted, my windows sealed, and still it seeps through the floorboards with its familiar stink, and here it is, in the bedroom, between the sheets. Between my skin and yours...

MAN A taste, sometimes only a half-remembered taste between our lips of something vaguely familiar - metallic like blood and bitter as shame.

WOMAN Vigilance that doesn't allow for rest...

MAN	...against a constant intruder...
WOMAN	...a spreading hemorrhage, an oil slick. Violation!
MAN	Violation! Trespasses in this territory...
WOMAN	- desecration.
BOTH	From this thief there is no luxury of sanctuary... (pause; pacing changes; words tumbling out and overlapping, sometimes simultaneous.)
MAN	Something about the vacant blue eyes, the lipstick mocking from the glossy pages of the girlie magazines we used to sneak a look at in the drugstore. Mmmmmmmm... No questions asked, no talking back, no reminders of the brown face, slanted eyes, large lips in the mirror. The door was locked and bolted; it isn't my fault!
WOMAN	...dark, mysterious, devastating... succulent, exotic morsel of dark meat. "Would you care for a bit of thigh?" Pale and immaculate, he offered to share his micro-waved luxury. Served me up a generous helping of nuclear power. Eat your heart out Snow-White.
MAN	The Ice Goddess... (lights snap to full, stark morning light, the woman and the man are on their bed, centre stage, awake now they look at each other.)
MAN	Good morning. (turns away abruptly)
WOMAN	Good morning. (also turning) What time is it?
MAN	10:15.
WOMAN	Shit. I meant to get up earlier.
MAN	Sure.
WOMAN	I did! (gets up huffily and goes to kitchen area to begin her dance of washing. She wears a light nightgown or a slip)
MAN	(reaches for her, then withdraws his hand and falls back onto bed; slowly begins to dress, socks first. His movements are ordinary but carry the precision of personal ritual.)

SCENE 2

(In kitchen area, Woman is washing herself, the gesture evolves into washing clothes, washing dishes, or other mundane daily activity. Her movements transform from one into the other. She speaks through the movement.)

WOMAN Crossing the frontier from sleep into wakefulness you first touch the borders, then enter the tourist trap of my colonized body; this body that I can barely remember belongs to me. Gaudy, numb and bloodless, a carcass from a wax museum in Niagara Falls. Am I the woman who fell from the Sky World? Changing Woman molding bloody clay from the soft underside of her breasts? Can you still hear the warnings of White Buffalo Calf Woman? The wails of the earth?

MAN (from the bed) What day is it? No, never mind. Let me be lost.

WOMAN Thursday.

MAN (groans; beat) ...and where is the testimony heard of the territory stolen from between our bodies? (on his feet engaged in ordinary daily tasks; work. He is engaged in the same kind of transformational gestures and we see their dual dance.)

WOMAN Evidence.

MAN Somewhere a woman screams. Who is she? Someone tell her to be quiet! (as if scolding a child) What's the matter with you?

WOMAN Just who do you think you are?

MAN (on his feet) You'll stand with your nose to the wall until I say you can move. Get those hands back up over your head!

WOMAN Stolen: a way of knowing passed from nipple to mouth; replaced by sterile latex.

MAN (agitated) A ripping sound of splitting skin, deep moaning comes from all directions. No... (he locates the sound coming from deep within the earth)

WOMAN It's garbage day. (pauses for response) Do you hear me?

MAN (with increasing hysteria) She's in such awful pain. Some body shut her up!

WOMAN I don't want to miss another garbage day. There are ants marching all over the kitchen. They obviously never heard of immigration laws. Roach prisons, ant traps, lemons on the back floor sill; and still they swarm.

(during Woman's last speech, Man rushes between kitchen and living room areas, with great anxiety, he puts some food on a plate, smudges it ceremonially and holds it out in front of him)

MAN I offer this... (pleading) Stop screaming! (begins to sing softly; a prayer; a mourning song)

WOMAN You see, first they send out a scout. Once the scout discovers where the food is, he transmits back to the rest of the ants, and that information forever becomes part of their ant memory. (sings) "The ants go marching one by one... Hurrah, hurrah..."
(Woman's last syllables blend into Man's song and they sing a bit together, weaving in and out of near laughter and near tears. Woman dresses while she sings.)

SCENE 3

(Living room area. In transition from previous scene, Woman breaks into a robust round dance beat.)

WOMAN (sings) "Travelling down this lonesome highway thumbing for a ride, Sure wish that pow-wows never end, way ya ha, way ya ha yo!" (raucous laughter) C'mon! C'mon, let's go to the pow-wow.

MAN Where's the party? You know what I heard?

WOMAN WHAT?

MAN I heard that pow-wow's fixed. They got their favorites, and they got their family and they win every time - even the ones that dance like turkeys making a milkshake.

WOMAN I know it! I coulda' won last year, 'cept for that head judge was crooked. They're all crooked.

MAN That's what I heard.

WOMAN That pow-wow princess, Minniehaha, all the time snapping eyes at me - cross-eyed thing - And trying to steal my moves!

MAN Who?

WOMAN You know the one! Don't try and tell me you didn't notice! The one with the neon fringes.

MAN I got better things to do than to watch you women scratch each other's eyes out. Had to watch my own back real good. Yeah. You see that one drum come in? Swaggering like their shit don't stink -

WOMAN - or like the nails are coming through their boots.

MAN Jeans so tight you'd swear they took a Brillo pad to the crotch just to wear 'em down. Don't tell me you didn't notice.

WOMAN (shrugs)

MAN A singer from one of the other drums lost his voice. Couldn't make a sound. Medicine wars.
WOMAN That's what I heard.
MAN (explodes) I should've kicked all their asses! Ground their teeth into the dirt - the whole damn family! Nobody messes with me! (screams) I'M A WARRIOR!
WOMAN A thief stalks the perimeter of the sacred hoop where the centre is not honored.
MAN (calm) Y'know, they don't have McDonald's in Newfoundland.
WOMAN No?
MAN Unh-unh, they're afraid of Micmac attacks.
WOMAN Oh, you...
MAN Wanna braid my hair?

(Their laughter folds into a very intense embrace on the edge of desperation. This first real connection between them resonates a common memory and they see themselves as who they might have been. The transition into the next scene starts from the embrace and all the strength, fear and duality within it. The transformation spans time.)

SCENE 4

(The next section is gestural; strong, clear, rhythmic movements describe the work of daily life in a pre-contact world: planting, fishing, gathering, hunting, caring for children, grinding corn, prayer, and ceremony. The man and woman work sometimes separately, sometimes together, but always in balance. Suddenly the Woman stops working and peers out as if trying to hear a faint sound. Her breathing becomes audible and rhythmically erratic.)

MAN What is it? What do you see?
WOMAN A floating house with huge wings coming out of the sunrise.
MAN There's a ship on the horizon.
(very slowly they draw closer to each other)
WOMAN (very quietly) ...soft as mist...
MAN ...a fast-growing mold...
WOMAN ...between my body and yours...
MAN ...bitter as shame.

(FADE)

World Compteition Dances

World competition dances
elite coming forward
begin where we stand
no big do
but shows who cares
who doesn't
for something NOT ours
don't squirm
where you stand
when the drums roll
relax, be one
but notice that one
as he dances like none before
with modern techniques
and
angry stomps
bring crowded cities
daring slashes
tear her dirt
wild turns
move her rivers
while those eyes
burn
hatred evil red
as we're shown
chemical swill
acid rain
animal extinction
ozone depletion
with his dance.
One has only
to glance
to judge

Arnie Louie

Survival

1. A small buck tenderly pulled the
nourishment from Mother Earth's breast. The
meadow hay danced with the wind along the
crest of the thawed mountains. Another day had
awakened creation to breathe. The feast
settled in the midst of growth under
the watchful eye of Grandfather Mountains.
A baby stood, nurtured and fenced in by the
endless bloom of spring.

2. The sun toasted the hillside along
Okanagan lake. Deep within the ocean
of sage and pine rested a two point
white tail. His coat blended well into
the tainted colours of summer. Hidden
from the eyes of traffic below. He was
safe for as long as his thirst could endure.

3. Autumn leaves scattered themselves across the
peaks and valleys of Coyote's land. Weathered
mountains hugged the grand waters of
paradise. Deep within the bosom of
life sleeps a seasoned buck and a spirit
sprouted from fertile grounds.

4. The rain fell hard against my naked
face. Unable to wash away a cold stare of
temper. A wintered breeze spashed off
a stricken corpse, as it lay still in
the night. An approaching vehicle
casted light upon the wounded animal
only to pass by without remorse.

Jameson Brant

451 : 49

The borrowed tools we use, the ones we think are going to make things easier but usually end up invoking seemingly infinite difficulty and premature grey hair.	:	The natural implements that we think we can't remember, yet weep for at the graves of our beloved.
The Perrier, Montclair and Vichy that stocks a small space on the refrigerator rack of every environmentally-conscious intellectual.	:	Cool, fresh water gathered at the source. The one that reminds us what the real On'nigo nohs is supposed to taste like.
The salt pork and the beef we use to flavour our corn soup, so carefully rinsed after the baking soda process.	:	The so-called savage beasts that the guys who thought they were in charge put on the endangered species list after centuries of bureaucratic rot.
The things that we're taught will work.	:	That which works.
The diseases that teach us to know fear.	:	The plants, the medicines and the know-how. A bundle neatly tucked somewhere.
Insomnia.	:	A power snooze.
Contraception. The ones we asked not to make it.	:	A cry in the night that we delight to and the peeping coo that we too once uttered.
The rebels who conformed, and even the ones who didn't.	:	The survivors. The ones who walk the talk
The time we spend getting there.	:	Being there.

Jamieson Brant

Conversations wasted on complaints about the weather, atmospheric complications and how much time we have left.	:	A ceremonial reminder of who we really are and how we fit in.
Languages spoken by the masses and all the names they decided to call us.	:	Words which make more sense to the earth-toned one who identifies himself when addressing the Creator and who still refers to himself as a human-being.
Borders, boundaries and bingo. Bush-like solutions, the ones that cost a lot of money convincing us that we're doing the right thing to balance the books.	:	Earthquakes, volcanic eruptions, floods and other labour-related pains suffered by the mother.
Industrial clouds and acid rains.	:	Dew, an early morning frost and spring break-up.
Soaring oil prices, hydro bills,	:	Our elder brother the Sun.
nuclear secrets, and fast-moving atoms to tempt the cold ones who greed.	:	The Gift and conversations carried on by the Firekeepers
Music to ignite jealously and other such inflations.	:	The creature's heartbeat.
The clock.	:	The drum.

451

ᐊᐸᒋᑕᐧᐃᓇ ᑲ ᔭᐧᐊᔪᐊᐸᒋᑕᔭᐠ,
ᑲ ᐃᑌᓂᑕᒪᐠ ᑭᒋ ᐧᐁᑎᔪᔭᐠ
ᐁ ᐊᐸᒋᑕᔭᐠ ᒪᑲ ᑲ ᐊᑎ
ᒪᓂᐸᓂᐃᑯᔭᐠ ᓄᐢᑕ ᐧᐃᐸᐨ
ᑲ ᐅᒋ ᐧᐊᐱᑎᐢᐧᑲᓇᓂᐧᐊᐠ.

ᓇᓇᑲᐤ ᑲ ᐃᓯ ᓂᑲᑌᑭ
ᓂᐱᔭ ᑲ ᐃᓯ ᐱᑕᐊᑭᐠ
ᑲ ᐅᓯᑕᒋᐠ ᑲᑕ ᐸᐦᑲᑲᒥᐧᓇ
ᑲ ᐃᑌᓂᑕᑭᐠ ᐃᐢᐱᐨ
ᐱᐧᐊᐱᐢᑯᐠ ᑲ ᐅᒋᐸᓂᐠ
ᐅᐅ ᒪᑲ ᓂᐱᔭ ᐱᐧᐊᐱᐢᑯᓇᑲᓂᐠ
ᑲ ᐱᒋᑎᑭ ᐁ ᑭ ᐸᐢᑌᑭ ᒪᑲ ᑲᑕᑲᐠ
ᑲᐸᑎᐠ ᐁ ᐊᐢᑕᓂᐧᐊᑭ.

ᑯᑯᐡ ᑲ ᓯᐧᐃᑕᑲᓂᐧᐃᐟ ᒥᐢᑐᔪᐧᐃᔭᐢ
ᑲ ᐊᐸᒋᑕᔭᐠ
ᑭᒋ ᐧᐃᑲᑲᒥᐠ ᑭ ᒧᐡᑲᒥᒥᓇᐤ
ᐁ ᐅᓯᑕᔭᐠ ᐊᓂᒋᒥᓂᔪᑊ
ᓄᐢᑕ ᐊᐧᐁᐣᑕᐠ ᑲ ᑭ ᑭᒋᐢᑎᐸᐧᐊᓂᑯᐠ
ᐊᓂᒋᒥᓇᐠ.

ᑲ ᑭ ᑭᐢᑭᓗᐊᒪᑲᐧᐃᔭᐠ
ᑫᐧᑲᓇ ᑲᑕ ᑭᐊᐸᑎᔪᒪᑲᐧᓇ
ᑲ ᑭ ᐃᑌᓂᒋᑲᑌᐠ.

ᐊᑯᔪᐧᐃᓇ ᑲ ᑭᐢᑭᓗᐊᒪᑯᔭᐠ
ᑫ ᐅᒋ ᓇᓂᒋᐢᑕᒪᐠ ᑫᐧᑲᐣ.

ᐁᑲ ᑲ ᑭᓂᐸᐟ ᐊᐧᐁᓂᑲᐣ.

ᓇᓇᑲᐤ ᑐᐧᐃ ᐣᑐᑯᓗᓇ ᐁᑲ
ᑫᐅᒋᐊᔭᐧᐃᐟ ᐊᐧᐊᓯᓴ
ᑲ ᑭ ᐃᐧᑌᔭᐠ ᐁᑲ ᑭᒋ
ᐅᓯᑕᓂᐧᐊᑭ.

ᒪᓯᑫᐧᐃᓂᓂᐧᐊᐠ ᑲ ᑭ
ᐣᑕᐧᐃ ᒪᓯᑫᒋᐠ ᐊᓂᑭ ᒪᑲ
ᓄᐢᑕ ᐁᑲ ᑲ ᐅᒋ ᑭᑐᑌᒋᐠ

49

ᒥᔪᐧᐁ ᑫᐧᑲᐣ ᒪᑲ ᑲ ᐃᑭᐠ
ᓂᐧᐊᓂᑭᐢᑭᔪᑐᑌᐣ ᑲ ᐃᑌᓂᑕᒪᐠ,
ᑭᔭᐱᐨ ᒪᑲ ᓴᑯᐨ ᑲᒪᑐᑐᑕᒪᐠ
ᑭᒋᐸᐃᑲᒥᑯᓇᐧᐊ.

ᑲᒪᐧᐊᑐᓂᑲᑌᐠ ᓂᐱᐣ ᑲᑕᑭᑲᒥᐠ
ᑲᐸᐦᑲᑲᒥᐠ.
ᑲ ᐧᐃᑕᒪᑯᔭᐠ ᑕᓄ ᐧᒣᒋ
ᐁᐢᐸᐧᑲᐠ ᐊᓂᒪ ᑕᐧᐯ ᑕᑭᐱᐣ.

ᐸᐧᑲᒋ ᐊᐧᐃᔭᓯᓴᐠ
ᐊᒥᐢᑯᑭᒪᐧᐊᐠ ᑲ ᑭ
ᐃᑌᓂᑕᑭᐠ ᐁᑎᐯᓂᒪᒋᐠ
ᑭᒋ ᐧᐁᐡᑲᐨ ᑲ ᑭ ᐅᒋ
ᐊᔭᒥᑐᑕᐧᐊᒋᐠ
ᐁᑲ ᑭᒋ ᓂᐸᐃᒥᒋ ᐁᑲ ᑭᒋ ᒐᑭ ᐃᒥᒋ.

ᑲ ᑭ ᐊᐸᑎᔪᒪᑲᐠ.

ᒥᔪᐧᐁ ᐸᐧᑲᑕᐢᑭᐠ ᑲ ᑭ
ᐅᑎᓂᑲᑌᑭ ᐣᑐᑯᓗᓇ.
ᑲ ᑭ ᐃᓯ ᑭᐢᑫᓂᒋᑲᑌᐠ
ᓄᐢᑕ ᑲ ᑭ ᓇᐃᑭᑲᑌᐠ
ᐊᓂᒪ ᒥᐧᐊᐟ ᑭᒋ ᐧᑲᔭᐢᐠ.

ᐁ ᑭᒋ ᑭᐢᑕᐸᑕᐠ ᐁᓂᐸᓂᐧᐊᐠ.

ᐊᐧᐊᓯᐡ ᐁᒪᑐᐟ ᒣᐧᑲᑎᐱᐢᐠ
ᐊᑕ ᒪᑲ ᑲᐸᐧᑲᔪᑕᐧᐊᐠ
ᓴᑯᐨ ᒪᑲ ᓄᐢᑕ ᐁᒥᐧᓄᓂᑕᒪᐠ
ᐁᐯᑕᐧᐊᐠ ᐁᒪᑐᐟ

ᒥᔪᐧᐁ ᐊᐧᐁᓂᑲᐣ ᑲ ᐱᒪᑎᔪᐟ
ᐊᓗᐨ ᑲ ᑭ ᐱᒪᒋᐅᒋᐠ.

Cree Translation by Angela Sisheesh

ᐃᓂᑯᐠ ᑲ ᑭ ᐃᐢᐸᓂᐃᑯᔭᐠ
ᑭᒋ ᑕᑯᔑᓂᔭᐠ ᑲ ᐧᐃ ᐃᑐᑌᔭᐠ

ᐸᐧᑲᐣᑕᐤ ᑲ ᐅᑕᒥᐧᐁᑕᓂᐊᐠ
ᐁᐊᔭᒥᑐᒋᑲᑌᐠ ᐁᔑᑭᔑᑲᐠ
ᑲᒪᓂᐸᓂᐃᐧᐁᒪᑲᐠ
ᑲᐅᑕᒥᐃᐧᐁᒪᑲᐠ

ᐃᔑᑭᐧᒐᐧᐃᓇ
ᑲ ᐊᔭᒧᐧᐊᑫᒋᐠ ᒥᑫᐟ
ᐊᐧᐁᓂᑲᓇᐠ ᑲ ᐊᐸᑎᓯᒋᐠ
ᓀᐢᑕ ᒥᓯᐧᐁ ᐃᔑᓂᑲᓯᐧᐃᓇ
ᑲ ᐃᑌᓂᑕᑭᐠ ᑭᒋ ᐃᔑᓂᑲᑎᑕᑯᐠ

ᐊᐢᑭᐠ ᐱᐣᑯᑫᐧᐃᐣ
ᒥᓯᐧᐁ ᓇᓇᑲᐤ ᑫᐧᑲᓇ
ᑲ ᐊᓂᒥᐃᑯᔭᐠ ᓀᐢᑕ
ᑲ ᒣᐢᒋᐸᓂᐃᑯᓇᓂᐧᐊᐠ
ᒪᑲ ᐁ ᓇᓇᐢᑯᐢᑕᑐᓇᓂᐧᐊᐠ
ᑲ ᐅᒋ ᐃᑌᓂᑕᒪᐠ ᒥᑐᓂ
ᐁ ᒪᒣᓄᔭᐠ ᐁᒥᓄᓇᑯᑕᔭᐠ
ᑭᓭᓂᔭᓇᓯᓇᐃᑲᓂᓇᐧᐊ᙮

ᐊᐸᑎᓯᐧᐃᑲᒥᑯᐠ
ᐸᐢᑌᐤ ᑲ ᐅᑕᐸᑌᐠ ᑲ ᐅᒋ
ᐱᒋᐧᐸᐱᓯᐟ ᑲᐦᑲᐧᐊᓇᐢᐠ
ᓀᐢᑕ ᑲ ᐅᒋ ᒪᓇᑕᐠ ᑭᒧᐧᐊᓇᐳᐣ

ᑲᑎᓇᑲᑭᑌᐠ ᐱᒥᐣ
ᐅᒥᓂᐢᑭᐧᐃᐦᑯᑌᐧᐃᒪᓯᓇᐃᑲᓇ
ᐸᑭᓯᑲᓂ ᑫᐧᑲᐣ ᑭᒧᑎᓯᐧᐃᐣ
ᓀᐢᑕ ᒥᓯᐧᐁ ᑫᐧᑲᐣ ᑲ ᐊᑎ
ᑲ ᑭᔑᐸᓂᐠ ᐁ ᐃᑭᐠ ᐊᑎᐟ ᒪᑲ
ᐁᑲ ᑲᓇᐁᓂᑕᑭᐠ ᐅᐅ ᑫᐧᑲᓇ ᑲ ᐃᑭᓂᓂᑭ
ᒥᓯᐧᐁ ᑫᐧᑲᐣ ᑲᓇᑲᑭᑌᐠ᙮

ᐱᓯᒧᑲᐣ᙮

ᐁ ᐃᑕᔭᐠ ᒪᑲ ᐊᐣᑕ᙮

ᒪᐧᐊᒋᐃᑐᐧᐃᐣ ᑲ ᐅᒋ
ᐧᐃᑕᒪᑯᔭᐠ ᑕᐣᑌ ᐧᐁᑕᐢᑲᓀᓯᔭᐠ
ᓀᐢᑕ ᑕᐣᑕ ᑲ ᐅᒋ ᑎᐯᐣᑕᑯᓯᔭᐠ

ᐊᓇ ᐅᑎᐧᑌᐧᐃᓇ ᑲ ᐊᔭᒥᐟ
ᑲᑕᐧᐯᒪᑲᓂᓂᑭ ᐁ ᑭᐢᑫᓂᑕᑯᐃᑎᓯᐟ
ᐃᐢᐱ ᐁ ᐊᓂᒧᒪᐟ ᑭᒋᒪᓂᑐᐧᐊ
ᓀᐢᑕ ᑭᔭᐱᐨ ᐃᓂᓂᐠ ᑲ ᐃᑕᑭᒥᑎᓯᐟ

ᑭᐧᑲᐧᓇ ᓀᐢᑕ ᑲ ᓂᐢᑭᐳᑌᐠ
ᓀᐢᑕ ᑯᑕᑭᔭ ᑫᐧᑲᓇ ᑲ ᐃᑭᑭ
ᐊᑐᐢᑫᐧᐃᓂᐠ ᑲ ᐅᒋ ᓇᓀᑲᑌᓂᒧᔭᐠ᙮

ᑫᑭᒐᐸᔭᓂᐦᑲᔭᐧᐊ
ᓀᐢᑕ ᐁᑎᓯᐧᑲᐠ᙮

ᓇᓇᑲᐤ ᐊᐧᐃᔭᔑᔕᐠ ᐅᐸᐸᑭᑌᐁᐧᐃᓂᐧᐊᐤ᙮

ᒪᐧᑌᐊᐢᑭᐧᑲᐣ᙮

We Remember

We Remember

Once fish swam
These great rivers
once the Buffalo roamed
these plains

We Remember

The little Child picked
blueberries while listening
to the whispers of the
cold wind.

We Remember

The fine lines
through the walk of life
leaving our mark

We Remember

the Great One
Who put us here
and will take us
back.

SUMMER

Sika'Dama-nox (Carla Robinson)

Being Alive

I look upwards to the daunting trees and whisper gently back to the wind. What is it trying to say to me? I wonder as I tip toe ever so gently on the moist dewy moss that ushers me into the womb of its forest. The magnificent cedar trees that loom over me scratch each other and welcome me to their humble abode. I see nothing humble about this mysterious unknown that I have visited many times before.

I take larger, more adventurous steps along a path, void of unfriendly thorn bushes. An eagle brother glides above me and watches me with unwelcoming eyes. No longer does he trust me, yet he never harms me. The trees again play their games, rubbing and tickling each other's massive bodies.

In the distance I can hear the ocean massaging the shore of the land. The water cools the smooth rocks and hums a tune only the ocean knows. Her scent beckons me, coos to me, and issues into my mind the memory of her tasty, salty flavour.

The moss and twigs help me move swiftly by giving me spring and stability. An aged tree has fallen over a gorge, lovingly, in its old age, knowing it would help all small animals trying to cross the hazardous valley. I carefully step over the elderly tree and thank him for being so thoughtful.

As I come closer to her, I can see more of the wide blue sky. Over a small ridge I can see her playful waves, smell her tangy breath, and feel her cool windy presence.

When I emerge from under the thicket of the forest, I can feel each pebble under my bare feet. They chatter and wonder what strange sensation they feel on top of themselves. I skip onto the logs spread horizontally along the beach and run gently along their backs. They creak and shuffle beneath me, it is a long time since they have had their backs scratched.

The ponds of sea water that have collected themselves in between the rocks after the last high tide are bathing in the warmth of the sunlight. I dip my feet into their shallow bodies and they envelope me with their gentle caresses. All who watch me know I have reached my destination. I spread my blanket over the smooth rock and gaze up to the wide skies and sing inwardly to my protectors the mountains. Happiness gurgles up from my soul and love warms my heart and thoughts.

Slowly the chorus begins, first with my friends the small birds, then the harmonious insects, the rubbing trees, the high pitched eagle's cries, the drum of the ocean and the melody of the wind. They prepare for my song which is dedicated to life and the seasons. I gently join in their harmony and we, with all our strength, love and voices, sing to a crescendo for one moment which seems to last forever. At this one moment in time I am a part of the forest in totality, I am no longer merely a human but a part of something indescribable. Now my eagle brother trusts me.

Muriel Williams

Untitled

In our depths, like the ocean——treasures
like a spring board, an up-current, launches us forward
when least, we verge, to die, we survive
we are, we find, alive,
and sometimes it's only this preparedness to die,
that enables us, to live, and we are prepared, to live.
We live as glass on tables, we reflect, as artists do
The coffee spills, the ashes of tobacco,
the crumbs of fortification, wiped clean,
we see the smear. We see the reflection of your—face,
of the living—room.
The occurrence, no assurance of tomorrow,
sunburst, we burst,
the shattered glass in all directions.
The pair, the studded.
Unknowing that lurks in thick carpeted rug.
We shower in our joys.
Our tears unwiped.
We lick clean our wounds as sure as joys tumble from your womb.
We lick spaces not heeded by none.
Yet we are,
we are—
the air currents that you breath.
Purple tongue, we kiss thee,
for it is but pleasure ——
that we take this pain,
again
and again.
We make it art,
and there by life may go on.
It is only with this pleasure that we take this pain
again
and again.
Hid-de-ous pain.
One moment,
the messages,
pass through,
our thoughts,
a confusion,
a mass of interconnections,
we pain—
on canvas,

on tongue,
on molecules.
Graves,
so that planted,
three trees,
grow,
our saviour thus born,
for that tree turns—into his cross.
Intrigued at the connection,
we burst—into flowers,
my mother's the sun.
Yours is the moon,
and we dance, together
and we play, together.
as all good children, should.

We like our connections. — We plant them wise.
We know the stars are our eyes,
thus the moon lite,
we dry our eyes,
we shine,
we put a smile on our faces...
even in full moon.
Evil to some,
planting day for one.

Our tongues collapsed,
and our songs sprung from trees instead.
Each sway of the wind,
our caress,
songs unsaid,—
we spooked ourselves,
when reality—came true!
Our challenge,
we prepared ourselves to die.
Instead,
we flourished,
for our lips... touched the ground.
seeds planted upon... by quakes of hooves
we ran to our places,
to watch the setting sun,
and after,
the rising one.

Dan Crank

Life Rhythms

Look into the brown faces
of the Navajos.
Our people, our culture, our survival.

See beyond the everyday doings
of the modern and the traditional.
Our clans, our ways, our selves.

Look yonder, ahead
to the year 2008
half a million strong, but still
tied to the land, the Keyah.

For in the land is reality
There is warmth, growth,
and bountifulness.
And all around, there are the life rhythms.
Like in a living room; plants stretch
to hear the pulse of the music.

See the Indians, today and in the year 2000,
celebrating
the music of the land.
For in the Keyah is peace and goodness.

Squint into the distances, into the hazy landscape.
Red is a nice colour
'cause red is reflection of the land
at first light and last sunlight.

Every man's heart beats with the land.
Beyond street pulse and electronic sounds,
we hear:
a hot, ringing summer silence,
drippling water in a stony brook,
a high breeze in the pine forest,
cool snowflakes falling softly on a cheek.

Dan Crank

The Indian In America

before given names, before racial games
there were peoples all over America
Lakota, Dine; true people names
to us, it was beyond the words

our land; tribal lands, all across
this wonderful keyah
from the rising sun to the setting
a good, half a year's travel
but it took the sun only one day

the people between the east and
west oceans
oh; the food, the different languages,
the beautiful life
it continues in the peoples' hearts

that is why we return to our past
we celebrate the new way in the old way
this is why our broken brothers and sisters
walk the cold city streets

they are wandering; trying to get back
to the west
where they were born and released
the journey is hard; too much chrome
and too many others calling this place home

Armand Garnet Ruffo

Excerpt from "Grey Owl: The Mystery of Archie Belaney

You haven't been to Biscotasing? Boy, are you in for a surprise.

Folks there — in Bisco that is — are the friendliest folks you'll ever meet, people who really know how to kick up their heels and live. Indians and whites alike. I mean everybody talks about Bisco — Hey! It's got a population of 200 or so —like it's the centre of the universe and for a Riverman maybe it is, on the headwaters of the Mississauga, Spanish, Mattagami and Groundhog Rivers, some of the wildest water known to man. It's the place where opportunity lives, and action. It's from where the canoe brigades leave.

And so one morning I tell my wife Angele I'll be gone for the summer — I'm off to find work — and from Temagami I start paddling some 75 miles due west. By this time not only have I learned how to handle a canoe (which doesn't mean I still don't have a lot to learn), but by now I can curse, drink, dance, make love, throw knives, and generally raise hell with the best of them. And that's exactly what I do — when out of the bush I whoop it up with the Boys, you know the regulars (and become pretty popular if I do say so myself). When in it, I stick close to the old timers - the Rivermen - and pick their brains. Learn as much as I can from them. Life is freedom in Bisco. So free I decide to stay and not go back to Temagami. During the winter I take to trapping and send a few dollars back to my wife. It's the least I can do. I mean I want to go back but...

Another winter comes and goes, and I'm back on the river and then... things happen which I've no control over. War breaks out in Europe. I get piss drunk and in trouble with the law. My girlfriend gets pregnant.

What to do? What else but get going, escape. The law, the women, the past, get rid of it all. Escape and join the Army. (Besides it's my patriotic duty.) It's the way out. The way to lose myself, while setting myself loose, like a canoe roaring down a tunnel of water. Someone who knows how to shoot, whose mother was an Apache, whose father was a Texas Ranger, can be useful in the Army. At least that's what I tell them.

Ron Welburn

Festival at Shorakappok

(Inwood Park, Upper Manhattan, September 14, 1991)

We arrived at Shorakappok, the sitting-down place, ready to stand, and its spirits helped us through this long day. This is a village again, Shorakappok, for a special time. Singers beat the drum, stories come alive, and electric music too makes an offering as we work. Feel the ancestors' strength this day. Their touch is vocal and sensate. They live here amidst burial places for their men and women and dogs and the sturgeon. They are strong here, speaking from white willows of the clouds and the river's edge, their whispers curling like sycamore bark. The emissary bees persist to tell of this village sticking into the river like a poised egret's neck. Across the bay that white plumed fisher studies the shallows all afternoon, alert and still, teaching a patience we've lost too soon. Gulls too play here, drifting above crowds, casually turning their heads left and right. Perhaps they know the caves where the Reckawawanc's people concealed themselves from the Mohawks only to flee down island to Dutch perfidy; caves filled with shells we covered our dead with for a while. Lost places still here, closed at N'ashaue-kuppi-ok, the closed-between place, closing sycamore around us here as we stand, trading ironies like the exchange for Manhattan. The spirits of this place listen and whisper and some of us know how standing amidst a crowd is for listening, then stepping aside to feel their breath in the leaves.

Renae Morriseau

Grandfather (Song)

Years have past since he spoke to me

of legends, songs, and dance.
How the eagle soars
and the owl dance.

He told me of the rivers and the streams
then he'd say these words to me:

CHORUS

Give me your hand
and walk with me awhile
I am an old man and

I need your smile

He sang me songs as we

walked along the beach.
Of a raven flying high,

Sun, Moon, and Sky.

He shared these songs and legends with me
Then he'd say these words to me

CHORUS

Give me your hand

and walk with me awhile

I am an old man and
I need your smile

Years have past since he spoke to me
of legends, songs and dance.

Symbols of the union

keep our dreams alive.
He told me o' the rivers and the streams.

Then he'd say these words to me:

CHORUS

Maurice Kenny

"Blue Jacket" (Excerpt)

for David Petty

The old man stood straight as though he faced a judge or jury, or possibly like a potentially mischievous child. Eighty, maybe a hundred. Almost timeless air about him. Ageless. It was early spring and yet his exposed flesh, face and hands, were bronzed. He wore a somewhat ragged black suit coat and baggy trousers which seemed not to have been pressed for many years. A single dark hair raised from a mole on his chin, determined and adamant.

"What you doin' in those blackberry brambles?"

Before he allowed me to answer, and without pause:

"I watch you closely."

Straight as Aaron's rod. Not necessarily tall to any extremity, but he stood thinly straight, a warrior, a match-stick, proud of his being and carriage.

"Yes, siree. I watch... very closely."

I could not help but notice his arms...sleeves rolled high to the elbows...were heavily covered with thick black hair. At the moment I paid little attention to, really, what appeared fur running the length of his flesh from wrists to elbows, but thinking back now the body hair should have been grey if not white for a man of his age. I seemed more struck by the glint, sharp penetrating, in his eyes rather than his hairy arms. My glance moved from his glint down across a wrinkled face to his shoes planted on the muddy ground. They were curious, the shoes, or sneaks rather, red, raspberry red, and oddly looked store-bought new, possibly worn that morning for the first time...as though he had just emerged from his winter house and wished to meet the new spring in a handsome manner.

It was early May, the ground was muddy, and I feared his new red sneaks would become readily soiled in the mud oozing, squishing water from his bulk, thin that it appeared. Behind his imposing figure I could not help but notice his tracks, prints...where he had walked in from the woods' cover. I looked again expecting to find moccasins, but no, the red sneaks were there on his somewhat small feet, each foot pointed outwards.

He stared me down, puzzled.

"You Indian, too?"

"Yes." I paused. "But not too much."

"Either you are Indian or you are not," he snapped. "Not a little, not a whole lot."

He demanded a more exacting reply.

"I'm Mohawk...a little," my feeble response.

"Aaaaah. I guessed you'd be Indian even if you are pale as the inside of a cucumber, or plucked chicken."

He seemed pleased even though my quantum wasn't much in his assessment. "I'm a big Seneca guy. What Clan?"

His chest flared. His eyes softened but brightened like the flame of a night candle. Pride shown on his lips.

Clan I thought. It had been years since I thought of clan. Seemed years since I thought of Indian and all that implied. Years since I had spoken with an Indian. Before I could answer:

"My mother was Bear Clan."

I replied my father was Turtle Clan...from Canada. My declaration was met with something akin to a scoff. He waved his hairy arms as if to dismiss me. "I should have thought so."

Before he could ask, I admitted that I had recently, only the day before, come into the area from Ohio, old Shawnee/Delaware territory.

"Delaware." A laugh circled the word. "Delaware. They are all women. We put skirts on them folks 200 years ago. Still wear 'em. 'Cause we never said those Delaware could take them off."

I had been associated with St. Margaret College near Columbus, Ohio, and was now newly appointed President of the local community college on the New York State Southern Tier at Jamestown. That day, that moment I was looking the country side over for a house that my wife, Helen, and I would be comfortable in for a few years, perhaps through retirement.

His mouth puckered at this information I volunteered. He wasn't much impressed, I could tell. "Teacher, huh." whispered through the puckered lips.

"So what you doin' in this here blackberry patch? It's the best in the whole state of New York and Pennsylvania. I come here every summer, every July to pick these berries...big as your thumb, round as a full moon, blue as a star. Oh! And sweet, sweet. Sweet enough to tempt all the animals to squabble. Yup, I pick every season."

There was some question in my mind as to what the house owner might have thought of this statement, picking his berries. I knew that that would not please me much should I purchase this place and move in. "The owner doesn't care," I asked?

"Not much...I guess."

He raised his right hand with two fingers formed as if to pluck a ripe berry from the bramble, the thorns gripping the cloth of his black jacket. I noticed long yellowed nails, thick hairs on the hand's knuckles.

"You gotta share...if you move into this house. He always did even if he didn't want to share. Birds know when to get here, ya know."

"Well, I'm only house-shopping. I've several houses to look at and my wife, well, she has the final decision on what we buy."

He had paid no attention to what I said.

"You gotta share. Don't be greedy. I'll share with you. I don't even know you. Here I am talking to a stranger that don't even live on this property. You will," he pronounced quite empathically. "An' I'll share. Don't be greedy...even if you ain't much Mohawk."

I had to smile.

"Been comin' down here for long time now. Probably won't stop comin' down even if you do buy this here house."

He patronized me.

Shifting his stance, water still squeezing out of the mud around his red sneaks, he assumed a superior attitude; "I talk a lot. But I got the right...at my age. And I can. I'm a big Seneca guy. Seneca folks like to talk. They say we're pretty good at it. We learned that in council. You can pick those berries...the blue, the black, the red...if you get up before the birds an' others. They'll out smart...everytime you think them berries are ripe and ready, and you got a can swinging at your belt-side. Well, they'll out smart. What kind, not-so-much-Indian, you say you was?"

I couldn't help but smile. He teased in good Iroquois fashion. He was testing.

"You a damn Catholic, too? You believe in Jesus Christ? You go to Sunday church? You know the prayer, the Book? You know what a Quacker are..."

He did not expect an answer. He wasn't really asking questions but making statements.

"My wife, Flower-who-sleeps-in-winter...hell, darn...that wasn't her name at all. Her white name. Her white name was Maud Parker. An' my name ain't Blue Jacket. I just made that up to scare you a little, stranger. You might think I was the famous Red Jacket...my ever-go-greatuncle. Remember him. He liked to talk a lot. They called him wind-bag, or He-that-Fills-the-air. Great man, my uncle. Remember him?

I couldn't agree more. Red Jacket's fame remained across the world as one of the greatest of orators. Every school child knew this fact.

What's your name, Not-so-much-Indian?" He didn't stop to hear my reply. "My Maud was the one who said I talked too much. If I worked the way I talked...I'd get the work done. Why hell, damn, I don't want to know your name. You got a name now. Not-so-much-Indian. I only wanna know if you'll share these blackberries when you buy this house. Share with the birds, an' the others.

He stared me down. Stood his ground, eyes piercing my very soul, or morality, or sense of fair play. But if I bought this house, this land, these couple of acres and which comes with the berry canes, then, why should I have to share with anything, birds or whatever. It was mine. I could let the bloody berry rot if I were so inclined. No? He wanted an answer. He was deadly serious. The comic had disappeared. The glint held no laughter now. I opened my mouth, but as the words slid off the tongue he turned and left, left me holding the words on my dry tongue, stymied. He disappeared. Sort of vanished in the dark tangle of woods beyond.

Straining, I caught a glimpse of him striding through the forest in one small clearing after another, hunched over, as if at any moment he would drop to all fours and amble away content in his purpose of the morning.

Chuckling with a small grin...almost of disbelief...I strode off from the thick wide berry patch rising out of the rich earth just off from a running creek not far from the house I was considering. Surely this creek, or brook held trout, rainbow, and tasty after sauteed in a frying pan. Trout was my second passion after blackberries.

It was true, a fact, I must admit honestly, candidly. I have a strong passion for blackberries. The most delicious of summer fruits, seed or no seed. Succulent, sweet as honey, healthy. I longed, now that I had seen this remarkable stand of canes, to stuff my stomach with these delectables. Old man Blue Jacket obviously had this same passion. I was consumed by it. I had never lived anyplace in the Americas where I was in complete possession of such a patch. Store bought berries never satisfied my passion, my abnormal craving for these berries. There are those who crave cigarettes or avocados, or orange juice, or even heavy gravies. Not I. My only flaw was the passion for these natural blackberries. A rustle in the bush beyond invaded my reverie. There sat a squirrel staring glassy-eyed at me. Its teeth grit together, but lips parted. He sat on his hind legs, tail furred behind him, his little claws empty of nut or acorn, or berry. The furry creature dropped his fore paws and stepped towards me, turned on a dime and scampered off into the thick brush. What was he trying to tell me. No, no...my brother does not talk to horses. Nonsense. Animals do not talk to humans, only cats that rub against your leg when hungry, or dogs that wag their tails when wanting to go out to hit the hydrant. But they don't speak...except through body movements, body language. That squirrel had nothing to say to me.

Coming through the woods, the stands of conifers and cedars, I could hear Blue Jacket's echo..."Don't be greedy." That would take some thinking. A major decision...should Helen and I buy this house. And I was going to pressure her into the purchase.

I was born and raised in the city; a crack in the Brooklyn cement. Crown Hill, but remember well my grandmother and old Granddad. Mr. Blue Jacket reminds me of Granddad. I can still vividly remember visiting the rez with summer moons on the waters, canoeing, fishing for lake bass, and brook trout. How could you forget the wild strawberries and the June festival, or going to the woods with Granddad in late July to pick luscious blackberries for Grandma's pies and jams. All those summer berries, the blue from the Adirondacks and particularly the elderberry and the wine Granddad brewed. He'd sneak me a tip from the tin cup out behind his stacked wood pile where Grandma couldn't see him. He'd mumble some special words, pour the wine with a wink as he handed the tin into my boy's hands and say, "Repeat after me, adowe, adowe. You must always remember to say adowe, thank you. Thank you for life taken and which you are about to drink or eat. An adowe to the Creator and that which had given up its life that you may live...Gift of elderberry, corn or opossum meat."

And I would repeat the adowe after him, thank you bush, thank you Creator, and then take one small sip of the wine, give him the empty tin cup and stagger toward the house under burning summer sun. Grandma taught the sun was brother, the moon Grand-mother, and all the fruits were sisters. Though I was born urban, Grandma and Granddad saw to it I learned a little, at least of the natural world, especially to respect all living things because they were relatives, and they too had their right in the sun the same as we humans.

My father had been an iron-worker as a young man, a Mohawk youth desperate for employment, without much of an education, perhaps two years of school, who needed to go to the states, the city, New York City to find a job in high steel. He liked that work, and worked hard at it. In time when he married he proved a good provider, a good saver. Grandma and Granddad had taught him well, too. Nights, instead of going to the bars for beers, he stayed home with my mom and tried to learn a little more from books. He'd say, "You'll never know when you'll need to use more learning." Saturday nights he'd take us to the movies. And after our Sunday bath and castor oil he'd take us out for ice cream or some such treat. Never much paid attention to church even though he had been baptised Catholic. Never put, as he would say, much stock in church-going. Best to pray alone in the woods or at the river edge. He always told me that he prayed on the high steel and that that was a good place to pray. Not out of fear...my father feared nothing, he was a true warrior and hunter...but how much closer could you get to the spirit world then there on a iron foundation of a sky-scraper. I guess he was a good man. I remember him generous and warm, though he could tease and test...yes, exactly like Mr. Blue Jacket, but never taunt, ridicule or slander. He was a good man. I wished he had lived.

Mom, my mother was a different story. Not that she wasn't a good woman and mother. She was. But she wasn't Indian. A full-blooded white woman, born and raised in the Brooklyn neighbourhood she lived in when she met my dad and where she eventually died. Crown Hill. She was Irish. My dad, Henry, always said she was more tribal than any Indian woman he knew...except his mother. She got fat, slowly, after he reached one day too high to grab a beam. She claimed there wasn't any reason anymore to stay thin and pretty. Her man had fallen from the heights and she didn't need another. Her big Mohawk wasn't there to appreciate her anymore. She ate chocolate and lots of buttered popcorn before the TV on the couch. She took a job...clerk in a dry-cleaner's store. And she never went back to the rez again. Nor did I after I was thirteen years old.

One night after I had graduated from high school we heard a knock at the apartment door. A man stood there with a manila envelope in his hand. Mom asked him in and gave him coffee at the kitchen table. I went to watch TV. They talked a long time, and when they had finished, and the man had left, and left the manila envelope on the table, Mom called me in. I went to college that fall, because the envelope contained a special insurance policy my Dad had taken out for me, for my education. It paid my tuition, and I worked nights in a drug store and sold aspirin, toothpaste and condoms to shy, scared men and boys who stumbled up to the counter when they requested rubbers. I wasn't embarrassed. It was my job. My night ended with mopping the floor. I got through my under-graduate years this way. Then grad school...a math major. I'd teach. My Dad would have approved of that, I think. I wasn't overly brilliant, an intellectual. Wasn't going to Wall St., didn't have either money or smarts for either law or medical school. I'd teach. Good career. And I liked kids, students. I have taught math in one minor college after another for all these years. I met, fell deeply in love with a very pretty girl, Helen Thorne, and have been happy since then. Like my Mom, Helen is a full-blooded white woman who gave me one son and one very beautiful daughter, who thankfully has the sparkle of my Dad's eyes, his coloring, his sensitivity and his smarts. Now both my children are in college and working nights. My good Helen shared all the difficulties, labors, heartaches. She has been a librarian all of our marriage. And is a great berry pie maker...just like my Grandma was.

Born and bred in Brooklyn, my mother didn't go berry picking. She didn't make elderberry wine. She didn't say adowe before she bought a ham to bake or vegetables to cook. She did buy pint baskets of cultured strawberries and we had terrific shortcakes. And she saw, when I was very young, that I spent summers on the rez with my grandparents, and it was my real college...living with Grandma and Granddad.. And where my passion for blackberries developed. Nearly everything I own is the color of crushed blackberries: socks, pants, ties, pyjamas, shirts, car-seat covers, my sleeping bag for camping, even pictures on my office walls are of canes and ripe berries with people picking. I demanded we name my daughter at birth Sweet Blackberry. Helen discouraged this. Later, Tammy thanked me graciously and profusely.

I had to stand there beside this house under consideration and laugh at poor Tammy being named Sweet Berry. Old Blue Jacket surely would appreciate that jest, that honor naming. But would Sweet Berry have been any worse than Dawn or Aurora, or just plain Agnes. Sweet Berry would have been a great name. Perhaps I can tease Tammy into naming her first girl child this. I doubt it.

When the last echo of Blue Jacket's voice and crunching in the mud had faded, I found myself facing the stand of woods, a wide spread of sugar maples laced with white birch, witchapple, a single spruce, a mixture of sycamore, beach and tamarack. A young oak leaned toward a white pine, and near the house several cedars stood gallantly against whatever winds might rush off the hills. A mere foot away a white trillium smiled up at me. A patch of wood sorel colored the darkness. For a brief moment my eyes deceived me for I thought I saw Blue Jacket standing pine-straight within the shadows of the woods, spying on me, the house, the patch.

I shrugged, turned with key in hand and approached the back door. Helen would want a fine report on what the actual house had to offer. After all, that was my mission that afternoon.

I inspected the interior. I was more than satisfied, I liked it sufficiently to bring my wife for approval. Three bedrooms, a study, bath and a half, and all the other usual rooms plus a small attic, large cellar, medium garden plot, a three mile drive from the college and town, and the closest neighbor on either side no less than a thousand feet from the line. Nothing really unusual. Built soon after World War II. Neither a murder nor mysterious ghost hung in the night shadows, or so I was led to believe..no bad spirit rambling through the rooms. Adequate for our needs. I knew Helen would enjoy the rhubarb patch...if the creatures allowed...beside the garden, the day lilies, lilac and her hours slaving over the newly planted tomatoes. What totally satisfied me was the study and of course the wide and deep swath of blackberry brambles...forgetting the black flies, mosquitoes and no see'ems.

There were also canes of raspberries on the property, a few black caps, a single current bush, obviously wild strawberries in the general vicinity and in the small woods beyond I could guess there would be blueberries and elderberries. I'd make the wine just like Granddad did those years back.

Being something of a prosaic man, or as I've been told, I cannot, dare not wax too lyrically. But...my heart leaps up when I behold...to quote Wordsworth...blackberry brambles. I could at that moment taste Helen's pies, and the ice cream I'd churn in our old ice bucket. Come July we'd be rich in berries and growing fat around the middle.

I returned to my motel and phoned Helen. She was so excited that she promised she'd drive in from Ohio the next day. I took an early supper in the local Denny's, went back to the room to read, and fell comfortably off to sleep early.

On rising I was somewhat bothered by my dream the night before: the berries were all picked, washed, Helen had them between crusts and I was storing them into the deep freezer. I had the count up to 221 when I woke in a hot sweat...remembering Helen's words and my response: "Did you pick them all?" "Yes, every last one of them." You didn't leave any for Mr. Blue Jacket?" "No. Only the berries dried by the sun." In all honesty, this did prick my conscience. Had I made him a promise. I couldn't recall. I simply could not remember. My dream was of greed.

My report to Helen satisfied her needs. When we visited the house and land-site, she agreed we would buy the place and have an enjoyable life there. When the kids emerged from study at Christmas we'd hang real red stockings from our fireplace.

A sylvan May afternoon, late, sun slowly wending through the incoming summer light. Stillness of twilight and yet light remained brilliant, silver, not a breeze in any pine. Nor rustle of some tiny animal. Perhaps a deer or raccoon stood off in the darkness below the birch or tamarack in the shadows. One bird sang...perhaps a thrush. I couldn't tell as I'm not a true bird-watcher. It seemed too early in the evening for a thrush. Not a ruffle of clouds in the sky. Nothing rippled, bent, shook, rattled or warbled. I had the feeling of home in this silence.

The Buick waited on my cinder drive. I boarded, turned on the ignition and glanced out the rear window to back out. Turning to face the windshield....there he was, standing straight as an arrow...handsome in age...peering directly into my heart. I backed out of the drive and raced off to pick up Helen at the town library.

She had approved. Found delights a MAN WOULD NEVER discover without a woman pointing those special delights out to his naked eye. She found more closet space, a hutch in the dining room, a dressing room off the master bedroom and others. She sang blissfully over the kitchen cabinets, whistled about the unusual bathroom tile; she nearly fell to her knees to kiss the parquet floors, waxed and polished. She loved the place and couldn't wait for the furniture to arrive from our last home. The garden plot she aaaaahh-ed about. The front and rear lawns were in decent shape and size. She imagined lovely summer lemonade parties on the backyard deck. She ignored my blackberry brambles. When I called attention...she growled.

"They're thorny."

She had no interest. I found it a lone joy.

"Must be a graveyard beyond those trees," she ventured.

"How would you know?"

"Those brambles are too heavy."

I allowed that suggestion to drop. Corpses feeding my berries.

"There is one there..." She was adamant.

While she ohhhh-ed over the new bright kitchen, I took a stroll through my woods. It was thick but not as deep as I had originally believed the stand to be. And Helen proved right again. There it was...an old Seneca graveyard reared behind the woods topping a sloping knoll beyond a rise of green hills. "But how did she know!"

"I just did. I could smell it. I sensed it was there. Call it women's intuition...if you must. Remember when your granddad died, and Jeff March, our neighbor. Didn't I tell you their deaths a week before the telegrams arrived."

"You're sixth sense."

Parker, Jemmison, Jamison, etc..I read and named the stones aloud. Weathered, chipped, some drooping, a few knocked over, names chiselled so lightly in time that names were fading. One short stone read a "B" and then blanks for the entire first word. More blanks, and then the last letter, a "T". The date read 18 and something that could have been a 2 and a 9.

Obviously an ancient site. No new headstones with fresh flowers. Satisfied with Helen's prediction, I ambled back to the kitchen and confessed to my wife her intuition hit it on the nail again. Over a beer, my imagination played with the blackberries, ripening, picking, eating.

ing. For safety's sake perhaps I should construct a fence around my brambles.

We moved into the house. It all took a good deal of time and energy to settle things into proper places. Helen was most difficult: things had to sit at just the right angle for effect, colors had to complement....such as the dining room rug had to match the wax grapes bowled on the table. Helen said it was good taste, breeding. Time disappeared. Temporarily I forgot my brambles, but way in the back of my thinking I hadn't forgotten them. I continued tasting their jam. From our bedroom window I had an excellent and clear view of the berry canes. While stretching for bathrobe and slippers I could sneak a peek.

One morning, to my interest but great surprise, I watched while stepping into my slippers, old Blue Jacket saunter through my brambles. He'd lift a cane and drop it; lift a cane and drop it; lift another cane, check it quickly and drop it. He must have lifted every cane there. I watched him close to half an hour then observed him move off into the woods. I knocked loudly on the glass pane but he ignored my tapping, stone deaf. The next morning I'd beat him. I was there waiting when his first foot stepped out of the shadows and put down on the mown lawn.

"Good morning, Mr. Blue Jacket." I think I shocked him.

"Oh yes. Good morning, Mr. a, a Mr. Not-so-much-Indian. Out for a morning hike. Keep in good shape that way."

"Yes, me, too." I replied grudgingly. Under my eyes, he was lifting the sprays and scanning the ripening process.

"Heard a bear crawling around last night."

"Oh! Where? Near here?" I questioned.

"Yes, up by my house there."

"Where is your house, Mr Blue Jacket?"

"Around up there some." He gestured to the hills up beyond the woods. His mysterious response did not fool me, nor did it or the gesture answer my question. "You live near here then?"

"Not far up there someplace near. Nice morning walk. Not far up there."

But not far up there where? He wasn't going to reveal his house. Perhaps he was afraid I'd stop by and disturb or maybe scare his wife, Flower-who-sleeps-in-winter. I wouldn't dream of calling on them without first an invitation or at least a phone call to announce my visit. I was city born. Thinking about it now I'm not sure if it is Indian...phone before dropping by. "Well, what do you think? Ready to pick soon?" Then I happened to remember that I had tramped all over those hills where he had pointed to his house, and I couldn't for the life of me recall a house on the hill.

"Yes, sir, ready to pick pretty soon. Gonna make some bellies happy. Ready soon. Now don't forget to share."

He turned his back to me as if I would not be one of the happy bellies, and he waved his hand good-bye as he disappeared into the dark woods. He did not give me a moment, a chance to explain my passion, my life-long dream to have a huge spray of my own of these luscious fruits, and that nothing would make me happier. His warning to share made me very un-nerved, down-right frightened. What could I do. Well, yes, relax and accept the inevitable, or, or....I could construct a fence. That afternoon I called the fence people and the next morning the enclosure was there in place.

That afternoon I strolled out into the backyard for a breath of air from working at my study desk on college papers, and, there was Mr. Blue Jacket smack in the middle of the brambles, lifting and checking and lifting. How could that old man have climbed over that fence. It was four feet high, AND he wasn't so tall that he could simply step over, tall that he was. I blinked and he was gone. I blinked again and he was there again, lifting and checking.

"Mr. Blue Jacket. What are you doing? How did you get in there?"

"Morning. Morning. Nice day today again. Berries are ripening nicely, no?"

I briskly marched to the shiny new fence. "How did you get inside my fence?"

"Oh! I just did somehow. These berries are real nice now. Real nice. Won't be long."

I was so un-nerved I continued to stare at him, probably open-mouthed. Words would not rise to meet this outrageous occasion. The sun was hot that morning. Some humidity in the air. And my feet planted by the new fence, I closed my eyes, shut them tightly as possible with the hope that when I opened them he would be gone, not there, that my imagination played tricks. I kept my eyes shut for several seconds and when I opened them up truly he was gone out from the enclosure and tramping through the woods.

"How? How did he do it, Helen?"

"I have no idea."

"Today's Tuesday. Yes? No? Yes. Alright."

This time he was standing on the outside leaning against my new fence.

"Mr. Not-So-much-Indian, I'll make a wager that these berries will be ready by Thursday at sunrise. Mark it sir. Sunrise. Thursday this. Some belly gonna be made very happy. Thursday this. Sunrise." He dropped a bramble pushing through the fence from his brown hand,

and marched off slowly into the woods, his back bent, stooped. Suddenly he stood in his usual straight stance, turned abruptly, raising his arm to point at the silver fence. "That won't help, much, Mr. Not-so-much-Indian. Won't help." He smiled showing old and yellow teeth.

Needless to say I was stunned. I actually believed he was going to pick the berries on the bramble which he had held in his hand. But the shocker was when he turned about with his threat. And I knew somehow he could climb the fence. How, I didn't know. But he had. A stool maybe. A stone. I was positive he planned to pick the berries. Hadn't he said on our first chat that I must share with the animals. I was, am willing to have a bird take a few, and some for the chipmunks or squirrels. But, he meant himself, of course. And I didn't mind, wouldn't mind giving the old man some. However, he said some bellies, plural. Did he mean his and mine, or...whose? I must work out a strategy...the fence was not going to work, to keep the "animals" out, and he could scale the fence. If the berries will be ready this Thursday, Sunrise, then I'll make sure I'm there first. Before sunrise. I'll save him a few. I won't be totally selfish. Share...some, a few...not many. They are mine. I own this land. But for all the world to hear, and I shouted, I'll be there in the brambles amidst the sprays long before sun-up when he places his ol' codger's foot near the first cane.

I went inside to the living-room where Helen was still arranging the furniture and hanging freshly laundered curtains.

"You are being silly. Plain silly. That old man isn't going to rob your darn berries. There are brambles all over the Southern Tier. He's not planning to out-smart you. Though the way you are acting he probably could. You're worse than a hen on a nest."

Helen was right, of course. Why would he steal all my blackberries. There are brambles all over the area, rich and thick canes heavy with fruit. He probably has his own patch near his house..."up there somewhere near." I was blind silly.

Tuesday passed uneventful. Then Wednesday dawned. The day was deathly quiet. I managed some work in my study with my eye slanted towards the backyard. No sign of Mr. Blue Jacket, not even a robin, let alone skunk or chipmunk. I spent the day answering letters to old friends and family. Soon Helen announced supper was ready, a fine steak, rare. She teased about it being fresh game and the meal turned into a guessing game.

"It's a good old fashion cow."

"Maybe. A deer peaked into the garden and I took good aim and now you have it on your plate." She giggled, her fork in the air, the tines stuck into bloody flesh. "Actually I think it tastes a little like porcupine, maybe bear. Yes, bear, I think."

The evening passed slowly, as they say like molasses in January. I thought bedtime would never come. I could barely read for excitement.

"Go to sleep. Turn off the light and stop mumbling. I can't keep my eyes closed for your growls."

Before going off to bed, I had left my garden shoes, my pants and work shirt on the chair near the bed. Suddenly I heard the alarm go off and it was still dark. I had slept after all. Yet dawn was not yet risen over those hills. I knew the old stones in the graveyard had not been warmed by the sunrise. They would still be dark as my backyard. Why was I thinking of the graveyard. Imagining pies and jams and shortcakes, etc., I stepped into my pants. Pulled up the white socks. Pushed into my work shoes, stood, draped my arms into the sleeves of the levi shirt. It was getting a little tight and would be considerably tighter after Helen baked the pies and cobblers. I was willing to suffer the consequences. I dressed quietly so as not to wake my wife. She'd have no sympathy. In fact, when I told her before bed my plan for the morning, she laughed outright in my startled face and cried out, I wasn't silly, I was certifiable crazy.

Downstairs, I made instant coffee. No time for perked. I disliked imitation coffee, imitation anything. I wanted the real thing.

Now I needed the brew and there was short time for the real. Half a cup down the gullet. A faint streak of light struck the low cloud cover. A cold black cloud. Rain. No sunshine. Good. That would keep Mr. Blue Jacket out of my patch. I didn't mind rain. I fetched the raincoat from the kitchen closet, reached for my flashlight on a shelf nearby...and a large water bucket. I'd win. I should have accepted his wager last Tuesday when he stood leaning against the fence...I found a pair of thin garden gloves. I was ready for victory, triumph. I was ready for my blackberries. All of them.

Dew glistened...morning spit, foam which we used to call rattlesnake spit...covered leaves of the brambles, and the spit hung like a human had passed through expectorating everywhere. I reached the first cane. A few bright pink berries clung to the stalk. No black. I moved left. The same. I moved right. Nothing at all. Not a single berry of any color or degree of ripeness. I moved deeper into the canes. Nothing...Nothing. Not a single dark globular of fruit. Nothing. Not pink nor red nor black. Light was approaching, moving up into the sky. I could see now without the need of the flashlight. Not watching my feet, I nearly stepped in a pile of scat. Still warm, almost steaming, fresh. Must be a rabbit. What else could manage the fence. Or a raccoon.

Rabbits do not make that sort of scat...cylindric like a dog. Must be raccoon or fox. We'd sighted plenty in the area, one or two in our backyard. Fox eat wild grapes. Raccoons eat anything. Near the fresh scat I discovered prints. Five toes and the ball of the foot on the left; five toes and the ball of the foot and the heel on the right. No shoes. Didn't Mr. Blue Jacket wear shoes when he came to make his periodic visits. Of course, he did. So why did he come here this morning barefooted. As the light from the rising sun increased, I could more clearly see that the prints...and they scurried throughout the brambles in the soft dew-moistened earth...the toes of which were somewhat odd. The big toe was in the wrong position for a human foot. Oh! My God! In the wrong place for human foot. It wasn't Mr. Blue Jacket...and it wasn't...Mr. Blue Jacket would never defecate here, in a berry patch.

I slid back to the house for my rifle. It well might be needed. The creature might still be there in the shadows of those woods, shadows lengthening across the patch. I had a most unwelcome friend, an uninvited. The brambles were high, a good growth this year after a strong rain and good run-off. Leaves large, canes high, high enough to hide him if he were bending over, picking. And he could climb my fence.

Rifle loaded, I returned to the yard. The sun had now risen. Clear clean light filled the air, seamed through the brambles. At the edge of the canes I noticed black fur caught on thorns. There were many tufts. I walked through the canes. In the interior, the brambles were completely naked of fruit, clean as a dog's breakfast dish, and flattened to the ground. Not a berry of any color. But tufts of fur were caught on spiky thorns. My canes were ten feet deep, at least, and take seconds to wade through. They were cleaned. Trampled. All clutching bits of black hairs.

I returned to the kitchen. Defeated. Helen was up, coffee perked, and she had bacon and pancakes working on the stove.

"Well, how many buckets of berries did you pick?"

I grumbled inaudible words. Some of which were curses.

The kitchen window had a decent view of the patch...if you looked kitty-corner as they say. I looked for fox, raccoon, or whatever creature or creatures who stole my blackberries, my precious berries. I couldn't take my sight away from the window. I ignored the coffee, and it was real coffee this time, and I ignored the food Helen encouraged me to eat. Then, just when I swore I spotted Mr. Blue Jacket in the canes behind the fence. I rushed from the table knocking over the creamery, spilled the coffee in its saucer. I banged through the screen door, and spilled into the yard. He was not there. An illusion. I'd had an illusion. Trick of the mind. Houdini of my imagination. Optical trick. My depression, my deep, deep disappointment, my painful and costly loss conspired to delude my vision. He was not there. Rubbing my eyes, I heard Helen calling from the kitchen screen door, imploring me to return to the table. My coffee was cooling, and the bacon and pancakes were frozen. Who cared. However, I did return to the house.

"What you think you saw? A blackberry moving out there. Dear, it was just a black bear. Or bears."

I glared hate.

"You know they're here. I'm sorry, darling...but that's exactly what it was. The way you tell it. Couldn't be anything but a bear."

"It was Mr. Blue Jacket, I tell you. The Old Seneca."

"No, dear. That old man couldn't climb your fence."

No response. I slurped the coffee. Her irony deserved nothing, certainly not an intelligent response.

Late afternoon having finished off class projects for the last semester to start the first week of September, I completed a letter to a former colleague and berry aficionado. It was then time for my daily stroll, a way of keeping the inner tube off the belly, airless and flattened. It didn't really do that much good, but I played the game each day. I got out an old walking stick which had belonged to Granddad, a canvas fishing hat I hadn't much used that summer, and put a package of sugarless gum in my shirt pocket, and left the house avoiding a talk with Helen who continued to smirk and laugh at me through-out the day. I didn't need her brand of humor, sarcasm. It wasn't funny...the loss of my berries.

Out back I skirted the fenced but broken canes, stumbled through the woods and hit for the hills now with the western sun shifting its declining rays on breath-like mounds. I could easily see the tops of the headstones. What was my destination. Only a few weeks before I'd been there on my walk. They stood straight. Now several were knocked over. Strangely, the grass and earth appeared disturbed near the one particular headstone which had been so difficult to read. B. and the T. and then 18 something and then something which looked like a 2 and an 8. This time it could be read clearly. Not to say I was utterly amazed. The stone had been smeared with black-purple juice. The carving stood broadly in the orange light of sundown. I stared, couldn't take my view away. I poked the broken pieces of the stone with my walking stick; lifting some tufts of loosened grass; pushed the tip of the stick against a wad of black fur. A Canadian Goose flew overhead; honked a signal to its followers and disappeared in the sky. Somewhere from afar I could hear a dog bark. Weirdly. Solemn. Prophetic. The dog howled.

It took a few minutes to find the tracks, prints, but yes there they were in the softened earth...the same prints that were on the loam of my blackberry patch. It was then I took a last look at the headstone. It read: "Blue Jacket" Seneca. 1829."

I ran down the hill fast as legs would carry. I dropped the walking stick; a tree limb caught the canvas hat. I reached the kitchen door. Slammed it shut. Bolted the lock. And stood leaning against the frame, heaving, pulling for breath.

Helen wandered into the room for the glass of water.

"What's wrong with you? You look like you've seen a bear."

There was no answer. What could I say to her. She'd laugh me into eternity.

I didn't sleep well that night.

The next morning on rising I called the fence company to come tear the fence down. They could keep the metal for scrap. When the men had finished the work and had pulled out of the drive with their truck, I went to the garage for a shovel and spade. In no time at all the ground was cleared and the plants stacked for a bonfire. I wiped the sweat from my brow and neck, and uttered a silent prayer. I was so pleased that I had not named my daughter Sweet Berry after all.

For the remainder of the summer I stuck to my study when not in my college office and kept the nose to the books.

One evening before dinner, Helen asked if I'd like to have a shortcake for dessert with dinner. "Raspberry," she said.

My abrupt answer was simple:

"No."

Kateri Damm

From Turtle Island To Aotearoa

(i - new arrival)

morning shatters
like ice in our lungs
shallow breaths hanging ragged
above our heads
the tent is swimming
As women men children
twist turn
in a joyous rush to feed together
nnichkiwenh and i emerge slowly
from our cocoons
spinning in transformation
but unlike the caterpillar
we carry hope in our dull heads
as we shake off our old selves
to join the waves of maori
lapping at the shore of the marae

(ii - answering a call)

yesterday
the convoy that was mattatua waka
led us eastward to this place
where i finally come to understand
being called from home by voices i do not recognize
(but perhaps my true ears heard them
carried on the wind
or my true eyes read them in driftwood
like messages in a bottle)
and now i am aware
of slow cautious steps taken
inside this gate
where songs of family lines are cast
like nets across a sea of faces

(iii - drifting)

my moccasins step timid
on this part of mother earth
waiting for the pounding of other like-covered feet
my ears swivel but cannot hear the spirits whispering
"so this is what it is to be
a stranger in another land" i think to myself as foot follows
foot

but feeling the pull of my ancestors i am like someone walking
against the current

while all the while
my head drifts slowly home
where i know the bending of the trees
and the sounds of undeveloped places
where my sister's children dream
and my grandparents' bones are cradled by ahki
where the lost spirits roam
and the heartbeat echoes
where my words are
(buried under rooks hidden in snow drifts
resting in flower beds
floating on clear bay waters
filling the forest)

here i am the quiet one
here i must reach across an ocean to find the right words

(iv - gathering stones)

once more under the moon
and the words of these people
do not jangle like jagged rocks in my head
the steady rhythmic pounding of voices
is wearing the sounds smooth
so that now the strength of the tide is apparent
even to one who stays close to the shore

tomorrow aotearoa will be waiting
with more gifts
and new stones to harvest
but tonight with only my own hollow thoughts for company
sleep overtakes me
carries to the place of dreams
every echoing sight and sound and smell

(v - an awakening)

the morning sky breaks
i wake
stretching into a new day
that yawns before me like a mother's child
i wake
peel off my blanket shell
to air so cool and gray
i retract and re-cover
listening as bits of conversation tell me
the house is awake

i am still
but my thoughts are bats in a cave
settling in dark corners of the room
as i sink deeper into the pillow
like a footprint in the sand

weeks from now
i will fall through the sky to turtle island
clutching a bit of papatuanuku in my fist
i will create a new beginning for myself
on the solid back of canada

(vi - long-distance connection)

now the day hangs directly overhead
and my sister's voice is sap running in my veins
though our words are nothing more than
leaves falling from sturdy limbs

feet firmly planted
i call for my sister's daughter
who pours out the drops of knowledge
she has gathered to share with me
so that suddenly i am a woman drinking under arid midday sun
thus revived i offer stories to her safe-keeping
showering with love the signs of new growth
later we are all embraced
by the child's grandmother my mother
who grows more and more like her mother before her
"everyone is fine" she says

the roots are well protected

(Vii - actionsong)

far into another aotearoa night
stories are told so the young ones will remember
in turn
i make simple gifts of gathered words
but if i could sing
i would sing songs of thanks
to all our relations who guide our steps
to the whakapapa whispered on the waves
to te maori who have not challenged my being here
or my attempts at poetry
to the earth winds sky water
to moon stars and sun
to creatures of land and air and sea

if i could dance my actions would say
what my voice cannot

(beginning)

now this i know:
tomorrow will bring another day of remembering and forgetting
already clouds are gathering
calling each other closer
tomorrow more rain will fall

and someday our union
will bear fruit on many branches

yes
maaba anishnaabe on aotearoa
maaba rain on fertile soil

maaba the tree of all trees
    so the story goes

How The Rainbow Came To Be

Once upon a time, a long time ago, the Earth was very young and new. There were no humans, nor animals.

Mother Earth was very busy watching over all the little root children, as well as the young stones.

She was so busy, she failed to notice that Sister Raincloud had not been by for several weeks.

The root children were restless, for they missed the raindrop children. Mother Earth called to Sister Raincloud and begged her to visit.

Sister Raincloud heard the invitation and rambled her way towards the Earth, carrying millions of raindrop children.

The raindrop children missed the root children also and were eager to join them in play.

Once in position, Sister Cloud opened her arms and the raindrops happily jumped towards Earth to be with their friends. .

All except one small raindrop, who kept going to the end of the line until he was the only one left.

Sister Cloud looked kindly upon the small one and said, "Off you go, the others are waiting for you." The small raindrop stepped to the edge and peered over, he was so frightened that he sat down and began to cry.

Between sobs he explained to Sister Cloud that Mother Earth was so far down and he couldn't jump .

Sister Cloud was troubled; she couldn't take the small raindrop back home and she wouldn't force him to jump either.

While she pondered the problem, the poor little raindrop cried silently into his hands.

All at once a wonderful idea came to Sister Cloud.

She closed her eyes and imagined all the beautiful colours that she'd seen on Earth. Bit by bit these colours came to her until she had enough to form a ball.

She called to the little raindrop and happily told him that he wouldn't have to jump. With all her strength she threw the coloured ball towards the Earth. The little raindrop uncovered his eyes and lo and behold, there was a wonderful coloured slide connecting the cloud to the Earth.

Sister Cloud tenderly placed the small raindrop on the top of the slide and he joyfully slid down to Earth and his friends.

From that day on, all the rainclouds carried the special coloured balls. So the next time you see the rainbow slide look closely and maybe you'll see a small raindrop gleefully sliding down.

Grandfather, Tree, Musical Instrument

Long ago, many years before the arrival of the white man, there was a man who spent his whole life as the laughing stock of the village. He was the only man in the village who could not sing or dance. Going to festivals and socials was especially rough on him. People bothered him so much, he was forced to leave. He went to live alone. He didn't know where he was going. He walked for days. One day, in the distance, he could see a giant tree. As he got closer, he stopped to gaze at this beautiful tree, it was also as if it were a dream. It grew strong and tall, everything about it was perfect. It was so beautiful he decided that this was the place for him to make his home. Each day he would climb high into the tree and gaze at the village he used to call home. One day while he was on the strongest and highest branch looking out at the village, the branch suddenly broke and he fell to the ground. He suffered two major injuries. One was a broken leg, the other a deep cut running the length of his leg.

He spent the next few weeks lying down in terrible pain. He broke two branches off and made splint to stabilize his leg. He kept putting fresh leaves on the wound to help soothe the pain. To keep his mind off of his wounds, he started carving into the big part of the broken branch, he didn't know what he was carving yet. As he got more into the woods, he thought this could become the best water drum ever made. As his drum got closer to being finished, he noticed that his leg was getting better. By the time the drum was ready for the water to be put in, his leg was ready to walk on. When he got up to walk to the nearby stream, he felt a certain something special about his leg. It actually felt better than ever before. He got to the stream and filled the drum, he completed the drum by cutting off a piece of his clothing to make the cover. He went back to his camp, took one more branch and carved the nicest drumstick ever. He figured if he couldn't sing or dance, he might as well own the fanciest drum and stick around. On the stick he carved the beautiful tree from which it came. Just to break it in, he practised singing songs, and dancing. To his surprise he could sing and dance just as well as the people back home, in fact even better. So now he had nothing to be ashamed of. He also wanted to show someone his new drum, stick, songs, and dance. He picked up his stuff, gave thanks to the tree and headed for home.

When he got home, there were all kinds of strange faces that he didn't recognize. Finally he met someone he knew and asked why all the strange faces? The village was having a big social that would last for days. People were laughing and making jokes saying, "What are you doing here? You can't sing or dance!". He also found it very funny because he knew he would have the last laugh.

He walked to the center of the field where the social was taking place. He could hear the laughter and the whispers as he prepared to sing and dance. Slowly he started to beat a rhythm on his drum and then a song came from his mouth. Suddenly there was no laughter, people began to stare in wonder. Others who had not been paying attention turned to see who was singing such a beautiful song. People joined in, they danced all day long into the night. People gathered all around him, even people who used to make fun of him, but he never reminded them of that. They were asking him where he learned to sing and dance. He told them the story about the tree and his leg. Some people believed him and others didn't. The ones who didn't believe him went out looking for the tree but always came back empty handed.

One of the people who believed in him was this very beautiful young woman, whom he had been in love with all of his life. She never knew because he was always too shy to tell her. That night he told her, she was very quiet, she didn't say anything. He figured he knew it was all too good to be true. He left and went back to his place in his longhouse. He felt too embarrassed to face her. One day about two weeks later, she approached him and told him that she felt the same way. When he asked her how come she didn't say anything when he told her, she said she felt too shy.

Many snows later, he was old and gray, the father and grandfather of a very large family, and a very prominent man in the village. One day he got very sick. He quickly sent for his strongest grandson to make him a drag stretcher and bring him to the tree to give it one more special thanks. No one had been to the tree since he was last there. He didn't have to tell his grandson where to go, the tree was almost pulling him there. When he got there, he felt the peace and beauty again, it was so peaceful, he told his grandson to leave him for a while. After his grandson left, he closed his eyes, and remembered when he first came there, how he felt, how the tree made his life so much easier to live. He felt at peace with himself.

His grandson returned a few days later, to find his dead grandfather. He prepared his body with his good clothes, buried him, then he headed back home. When he got home, people were asking him where his grandfather was. All he could say was that he was dead and buried at his favorite place on earth. People went looking to try and find the tree to pay their last respects to him, but nobody has ever found it since - not even his own grandson who brought him there.

Fruit Tree of Life

In a forested area on the borderline of Canada and the United States there is a small pasture no larger than a football field. In the center of this pasture there is a unique and extraordinary tree. This tree bears fruit which is said to be the most delicious on earth. The branches of this tree would make the strongest bows and straightest arrows and spears for any hunter make any beaver's dam invincible or make a man's house waterproof. All that is said about the tree is legend, because no man or animal has attempted to break a branch or pluck its fruit out of respect. It is also known by man and animals that if the tree is disturbed total destruction of the earth would occur. When the tree is looked at, you do not see destruction but only beauty and peace. In the forest, just off the side of the pasture, there is a small log cabin where an elderly Cree man lives. In front of the cabin, there is a pen with a couple of chickens and a small garden.

Every day this elderly man would take his flute and go sit beneath the tree and blow tunes. These tunes would bring peace to any man or animal. Every note was blown perfectly without mistake, for if there was one foul note or mistake, destruction would occur. The old man knew he was growing old and it was time to pass on his job as the caretaker of the tree. He wrote a letter to his grandson from Wakmalaseet encouraging him to come visit. He said that he had a job for him which required a great deal of concentration and responsibility. He also felt he was the only grandson capable of doing this job.

The grandson did not write back but he showed up two weeks later with a satchel full of clothes and a cylindrical piece of wood which he had been carving. He was ready and prepared to stay and do whatever work his grandfather had for him.

They greeted each other and the grandfather immediately started him doing chores such as feeding the animals, shovelling animals' droppings, and taking care of the animals. This happened every day, and every day the boy grew tired and slept for long hours. During his sleep he woke up to the beautiful tunes of his grandfather's flute.

The grandfather sat beneath the tree every day playing his flute perfectly. After a couple of weeks the boy had finished carving his piece of wood into a flute. He began to sit with his grandfather beneath the tree learning how to play the flute. After a couple of months the boy was playing his flute almost as well as his grandfather.

The grandfather told his grandson that he would die soon and, when that day came it would be he that would have to play his flute and charm the tree. He also told him that when he died he should not bury his body, leave him beneath the tree. He gave him no reason.

The boy continued to learn to play his flute until he could play it perfectly.

One morning the boy woke up late to hear his grandfather who was beneath the tree playing his flute, but it was a tune he has never heard before. He questioned his grandfather about the strange tune. His grandfather did not answer.

The next morning the boy awoke to see his grandfather lying beneath the tree. He went out to see what the problem was, only to find that his grandfather had passed away during the night. The boy went on with his daily chores, leaving his grandfather's body beneath the tree as he had wished. The boy had one more chore and that was to play his flute beneath the tree. After that was over he went to bed. The next day he woke up, and went over to the tree. He had noticed something was different - there was another fruit on the tree with a different color and shape. He then realized that his grandfather's body had disappeared.

It is said that this place still exists but only the Indian people know about it. You cannot see this place on a map and it is impossible to find. It is a beautiful place and would be nice to see but the caretakers fear that the white man would do something foolish and disturb the tree.

Mary Lou C. Debessige

Standing Beside Me

I am not here to entertain you. I am not here to tell you how fabulous everything is. I am here to tell you what I am feeling and how I see life transform before my eyes.

Today I see "clear cuts" everywhere. It's devastated murder, left by a foreign culture. Let me remind and tell you it is us they kill and destroy. These words may sound harsh and they are. It is also my reality because I come from both cultures and ancestry. First of all I come from a Native upbringing with non-Native destroyer of life influence. This also means my way of life on paradise Turtle Island is constantly turned into wasted lands by a foreign culture.

It is easy to blame because I've already learned foreigners' destructive behavioural patterns. I get caught up with other writers at En'owkin International Writing School by firing pen written notes and share my writings with others. I accuse the foreign culture of appropriation - stealing my voice, symbols and everything else imaginable. This leaves a disrespectful chaos. Where is my genuine connection to others? I guess it just isn't there.

So I have to tell you an important part of me that needs reconnecting. I find it difficult talking about the white-side of me. Indeed it is a sensitive issue for me because it makes me feel ashamed to admit I have a destroyer planted in my being.

Of course I've learned all of this conditioning as a child. It comes from a foreign culture's systems. This does not leave or eliminate destroyer potential in me so I've learned something very important. I had to learn to deviate from this foreign culture's system. I do not want to represent this unimaginable killer. I am honest when I say I am not proud to be part of that destructive system that destroys Mother Earth. So I've learned not to participate in the white side of my being.

I have a brighter side of me as well. I am also a First Nations person. This is the part that sustains who I truly am. I would forever like to be considered Odawa First nations, by this noble race. My Native side questions. What can I tell you that has not been told to you before about spiritual values? You've never listened to me in the past 500 years. I believe in the midst of all this turmoil and bitterness that there's a sense of hope because some foreign cultures are picking up lessons from First Nation's positive teachings. One of my ancient Native Ancestor's teachings says, to live side by side in harmony with nature on paradise Turtle Island comes natural to a spiritual being.

Another Native teaching is to pick only what you need and not be greedy like the foreign culture who destroys everything they put their hands on, including trees. No one needs to destroy everything anymore. This includes the other side of me. There are endless life cycles returning to allow us to learn about the "true value of one life spirit" that everything carries. Therefore I am part of the "clear cuts" symbolically represented as one main change to take place on Mother Earth. I can no longer be killed by the foreign culture because they've already killed themselves. I am here to help them to help themselves be resurrected.

I am part of Earth Mother and you cannot deny this fact from me any longer. On the other hand no one owns anything because all is for everyone who respect and share wisely.

In closing I'd like to share a poem with you:

Trees are part of earth our Earth Mother
Trees have always talked to me
They whisper gently in my ears
I relate to trees am a tree at times
Trees share my life fulfillment
& bloom in early spring
medicine wheels come from trees and forever turn
Trees teach importance of life I share with others
It is my spiritual responsibility to respect myself
This includes deadly lost foreign culture that cut trees
The foreign cultures are in contaminated journeys
Still life's on my side I feel compassion
My ancestors watch over my actions words deeds
My part is good, red road leading to eternal
balanced harmony
My sacred life flourishes in time immemorial

Kim Blaeser

Where Was I That Day?

It wasn't just the pill bugs

gray, many-legged and pulling that stunt
like they always did
closing in on themselves
contracting into the tiny round mass

like an image of the origin circle
And it wasn't the turtle alone either

who became so neatly one half of the earth's sphere

It was partly that day when I stopped at the little creek
and noticed the funny bumps on that floating log
and how they seemed to be looking at me
and how they were really little heads with beady bulging eyes
and how when I came back a half an hour later
the bumps had been rearranged on that log

It was partly the butterflies that would materialize
out of the flower blossoms
and the deer that appeared and disappeared into the forest
while standing stalk still
whose shape would be invisible one minute

and would stand out clearly the next
like the image in one of the connect-the-dot puzzles
It was the stick bugs, the chameleon
the snakes that became branches
the opossum who was dead then suddenly alive
And it was me who fit and saw one minute so clearly
and then stumbled blind the next
that made me think we are all always finding our place
in the great sphere of creation
that made me know I could learn a way
to pull the world around me too
to color myself with earth and air and water
and so become indistinguishable
to match my breath to the one
to pulse in and out with the mystery
to be both still and wildly alive in the same moment

to be strangely absent from myself

and yet feel large as all creation
to know
to know
to know and to belong
while the spell holds
learning to hold it a little longer each time
That's where I was that day
I watched you from the arbor
never blinking
while you looked all about for me
and then turned back home
thinking to find me in another place
when I was there everywhere you looked

I knew then the stories about Geronimo were true
and that he did turn to stone
while the cavalries passed him by
mistook him for just a part of the mountain
when he had really become the whole mountain

and all the air they breathed
and even the dust beneath their horse's hooves

I walk about trying to find the place I was that day
but getting there seems harder now
I feel heavier, my spirit weighted down
and I'm thinking I must shed something

like the animals shed their hair or skin
lose even their antlers annually
while I hold on to everything
and I'm thinking I must change my colors
like the rabbit, the ptarmigan, the weasel
and I'm thinking I must spin a cocoon
grow wings and learn to fly
and I'm thinking I must hibernate and fast
feed off my own excess for a season
and then perhaps emerge
in the place I was that day

and stay there longer this time

And I walk about and watch the creatures
the tree toads becoming and unbecoming a part of the trunk
the rocks in my path that crack open into grasshoppers and fly away
the spider who hangs suspended before me
and then disappears into thin air
and I feel comforted
knowing we are all

in this puzzle together
knowing we are all just learning
to hold the spell
a little longer
each time

Leona Hammerton

Sacred Union

That weekend
we set up tent
at the base of Pyramid Mountain
ate campfire cooking
drank black coffee content
as the fire's sparks
attempted to reach the stars
that weekend
we talked long into the night
and listened to animal sounds
and the Ashnola River lulled us to sleep
that weekend
we climbed to where pinecones
grew purple in abundance
and to where graceful birds
circled and taught us
of their perfection
that weekend
we shared papaya and sunflowers seeds
by a creek bed
shared hopes and dreams

and gentle laughter
we drank glacier waters
and I bathed prayerfully
and cleansed a painful past
to become reborn
into a magical time
of our own creation
that weekend
a butterfly
set its feet trustingly
on one of Your gentle hands
landed fleetingly
on my naked stomach
where my love lay gentle and grew there
That weekend
we joined bodies in a rainstorm
where even the thunder
was reverent

and spoke to us of blessed union
and lightning
danced playfully
sending power throughout the mountain tops
and deep into Earths surface
where Earth joins sky
where our hearts met and mingled
where our laughter
joy unfolded - took flight that weekend
memory in Earths history recorded
every rock and tree and grass
bore witness
a part
you and me

Heather Ahtone

KO

You rise on the horizon
Headdresses falling with horse's stride
Dust cloud shrouds force of
Warriors lining the horizon
Extending on rim of sun
Silhouette hides only your face
Approach shows eyes   Raining
You join Grandmother
Watch me for a time
We walk together
Fingers intwined
Suddenly to realize
You are no longer there
My prayer honors your tradition
Walking direction of Sun's journey
Striding to keep step
Day into night
Your shadow on the moon
Touch Step   Touch Step
Drum   Guides me
To sleep   To you
We laugh   Talk
Guide me   Still
Holding   My hand
Leading   Me on

Heather Ahtone

Two Eagles

My uncle said he saw the eagles, two, fly overhead as he prayed to the Creator. I didn't see them - but then I wasn't looking up. I could only see the blood - tracing stains on the breasts of the dancers - eyes closed to the sun - feet alternating in time with the drum. My hands trembled against the stillness of my will of a thousand years passed down by the ghosts of my ancestors - to this moment - two years ago.

My urbanized eye - so used to the bloodshed common in the city of angels - begged me to turn away. But they were held in place by a once dormant spirit - surfacing at the call of the drum. Blood pulsating from pride kept rhythm with the left step.

I found myself praying openly with a voice I did not recognize as my own - encouraged by the song of a man sitting by the south entrance. The Holy Man approached. I wanted him to stop - recognize me from a battle fought before the white man came. Holding my head high with soft eyes - I watched him pass by without a glance.

I reproached myself for such shameless folly and asked forgiveness - the drum offered consolation. I looked in time to see the ropes snap - my uncle fall to the ground. A breath escaped as a wave of humility engulfed me.

I stepped away from the arbor and walked to the empty field of sage. I felt proud that these were my people and humble as one learning to speak to the Creator for the first time - my heartbeat keeping time with the drum. I looked to the horizon with fresh eyes and a fresh spirit and there they were - two eagles dancing.

Charmaine Peal

Indian Dancing

Native people
Nisga'a Ceremonial Dancers
Red and black regalia
Button blankets with clans on the back

Beautiful, powerful, drums, rattles
beating of a heart
singing at the top of my lungs
Bodies dancing and rejoicing
smiling, sharing

This is who I am
as you look at me for the first time

Chiefs, warriors, drummers
women and children
happy, fun, proud
singing Nisga'a songs
Performing for people
making people feel good

I feel like I have no fear
nothing to worry about
sweating
all my worried thoughts and troubles
away
to be with the spirits

I am young
The smell is vibrant and awake
it's alive

Showing what being Nisga'a is
where we came from
the wars we fought

We sing the peace song
People watch with great interest
Kids dance with excitement
Family and friends we together as one

I cry because I am happy
I want to do it again
to feel the rhythm and beauty

Judith Mountain Leaf Volborth

They Came To Dance (In honour of Anna Mae)

Grandmother turned her eyes to me
and began to speak:

Not far from here is a place
where many of my children lie.
After many great wars with the blue-shirts
the People were without spirit and in despair.
A peaceful Paiute dreamer
told of his vision.
He said that he heard the voice of the Great Mystery.
That the Great Mystery would return the buffalo,
that there would again be plenty of nuts and berries,
that relatives, and loved ones gone South would return,
and that the Mother would open up with a whirlwind
and swallow all the wasicun, the small-eyes, and fat-takers.
But he said to please the Great Mystery
the People should dance.
And so it was the Ghost Dance.
The People came from all over
to share in this dream.
Many of the People were there,
they came to dance.

The Shoshones, the Cheyenne, and the Lakota,
they were all there.
They came to dance.
They used the sacred colors,
luta and ska,
they used the sacred grass,
to make the buffalo's return great.

They made shirts to protect themselves.
against the bullets of the blue-shirts.
On these shirts, painted in Earth colors,
were the sacred signs; Thunderbirds, Suns, Moons, stars.
They were all there.

And in their sacred Ghost Shirts
they danced.
And in their sacred Ghost Shirts
they chanted.
Yellow-Bird blew on his
Eagle-bone whistle.
The Circle grew larger and larger,
the chants louder and louder.
And the Eagle-bone whistle
would not remain silent.

But the blue-shirts
understood nothing.
Their ignorance quickly
Grew into fear.
They made the People stop dancing,
they tried to sever their spirit.
They herded the People into a Circle,
and surrounded them with four lightning-guns.
"Did they know of the sacred numbers?"
I think not.

While they had their lightning-guns
on the People
the blue-shirts began hacking apart tipis,
and ripping apart medicine bundles.
Yellow-Bird began to chant,
many eyebrows were raised,
the blue-shirts panicked.
Suddenly a shot-
then cracks of lightning burst out.
A Medicine Man threw a handful of dust
into the air,
and the lightning-guns began crackling,
pouring their bullets into the dreamers,
ripping away their sacred Ghost shirts.
Among the smoke and blood
the screams of women, and children

The blue-shirts quickly went about
robbing the dead dreamers
of their sacred Ghost shirts
and medicine bundles.

And it was then that a cleansing wind came,
and snow began to fall,
so the blue-shirrs left.

When they returned, after the blizzard,
they found my children
frozen to the Earth.

They pried the dead dreamers loose,
leaving behind
large pieces of flesh and hair
still frozen to the Earth,
and buried them
all together
in a large pit.

All close together
they lie in the Sacred womb
of their Mother.

They came to dance
at this place called Wounded Knee.
They came to dance.

Hetchetu Aloh!

FALL

Antoine Mountain

Harvest Moon

Grandma sits
In trees of falling shadows
A quiet sculpture
Gently swaying
To the lullabye breeze
The setting sun warms
   her tired feet
And bathes
   her creaking back

The ghostly brush of time
Drew her lines
   that run in tears
   rivers and trails
That others follow

With her sit
Her birth,
A life
   of pain
   and laughter
Pictures
With many different frames
A gallery
   of dreams

Yet, in all
A quiet smile
Is her mirror
The darkening night
Her quilted blanket

Feathered Dawn

Migrating geese song
Weaves a tapestry
High over ringing spruce
And drops of sunlight

Wings of Fall
Through September air

Richard Van Camp

Autumn's Silent Rage

My given name
roughly translated
is one-foot-in heaven
I was once a great leader
a rock
I raised warriors and hunters
I provided for my people
I gave everything to the tribe
and asked nothing in return

But lately asking's all I seem to do
Where are my children?
Where is my family?
What has happened to the great tribes?
who never lost battles and were feared far and wide
What has happened to the land?
For now it weeps and bleeds

What has happened to me?
the once great leader
for now I sit alone
for now I sit alone

I have a new name now
it's a name I've given myself
roughly translated
I am one-foot-in-hell

Jennifer Tsun

Search For Home

When the men
are drumming
late into the night
when the dawn singer
calls us
to sunrise ceremony
when we pray
together
speaking in ancient tongue
smoking grandfather pipe
the Circle is strong.

Then I have some
strength:
I feel my time for
sweat lodge
is coming....

At the gatherings
Everyone is smiling
connected
Family
I am a distant cousin
on the edges
a little chilly
out here.

I am struggling
to re-enter
the arms
the womb!
of Mother Earth
to sit in silence
and hear
what words can never
say.

Jennifer Tsun

One and Two

One sunrise ceremony
One sun
One day
One little Indian:
Newcomer people, uneasy
want her to be
one white woman
But bones
of her aboriginal foremothers
lie beneath her feet
their spirits calling to the
red in her bones
living yet in her blood
in her heartbeat
She stands, a warrior
with sweetgrass in hand
she doesn't even own
a pair of moccasins
some hand-me-down
sneakers
single mother on welfare
sending prayers
upon smoke
of sweetgrass
soothes her rage for
a moment

Abruptly
she turns to the left
to the north:
Two young deer
watching
intrigued
two, not one, not three
two together
one wanting to move
shyly forward
dips head to the ground
almost takes another step
toward her

Jennifer Tsun

One and Two

The other whispers
nose to shoulder
"No, I don't trust
those two-legged ones."
They are bound
together
one cannot move forward
without the other.....

Head to ground, bowing
trying to pull the other along
"No, she's looking at us."
"But she doesn't have a long stick."
"No, I say, no."
She is as spellbound
as they
Then she sucks lips together
as one would call horse or dog
The enchanted two bound away
Thunder, she feels through the Earth:
You'll not tame us
like horse or dog!
She completes her prayers
for the people

Next two days
she returns to the same place
as if
she could see them again
hold that dream moment once again
Her nose is assailed
by cowshit vapours
heavy, cloying
she is repelled: ...
this is not a good place
to pray today
she goes home
indoors to pray
Always it's just a house
sometimes her sanctuary
sometimes her prison

Jeannette Armstrong

Reclaiming Earth

for my father Ma'kwala (Stone Hand Knife) who attained freedom from the body March 15, 1992

the jingle of spur rowels
and wagon wheels
across Blue Horse tracks
and pages
of hand drawn star maps
traced paths in parchment
pinpoint slits in painted rawhide
open to the moment
to slip the skin
away
to shake loose
the cocoon of organic being
encasing
clusters of incessant musings

the dreaming body
drops from the mastering of intent
caught in the force of absolute alignment
requiring the internal mouthing of sound
be stopped

the moment tightens
into fusion
transparent wings of incandescence
flash
then sink
mirror deep into violet
a light swift fluttering
into spots of jet blackness

a pure motion
clean
sure
speaking instantly
to rocks
trees
and eagle emanations
reclaiming

sky
earth
and stars

we wore eagle down
drummed the horse riding song
scanned the eastern sky
catching the glint of hooves touching milk dusty paths
and cheered
our feet holding heavy
to earth surface

Jeannette Armstrong

Grandmothers

In the part of me that was always there
grandmothers
are speaking to me
the grandmothers in whose voices
I nestle
and draw nourishment from
voices speaking to me
in early morning light
glinting off water
speaking to me in fragile green
pushing upward
groping sun and warmth
pulling earth's breath
down and in
to join with porous stone
speaking to me
out of thick forest
in majestic rises to sheer
blue
in the straight slight mist
in twigs and fur
skin and blood
moon and movement
feathers stroking elegant curves against wind
silent unseen bits
in the torrent of blood
washing bone and flesh
earth's pieces
the joining of winds
to rock
igniting white fire
lighting dark places
and rousing
the sleeping moment
caught in pollen
a waking of stars
inside
and when blue fire
slants to touch this water
I lift my eyes
and know I am seed
and shooting green

and words
in this hollow
I am
night glittering
the wind and silence
I am vastness
stretching to the sun
I am this moment
earth mind
I can be nothing else
the joining of breath to sand
by water and fire
the mother body
and yet
I am small
a mote of dust
hardly here
unbearably without anything
to hold me
but the voices
of gradmothers

Jack Forbes

America Before the United States

There was an America
before there was a United States
and we remember it.

We remember that it was
a land of pure, clear streams
of fresh, clean air
and landscapes of
exquisite beauty
and awesome reach.

We remember that
there was an America
before there was a Spanish Empire
before Hispanic Imperialism
devastated our peoples
and tore open Mother Earth
for gold.

We remember that
there was an America
before any European empires arrived,
a land stretching from
Arctic to Antarctic
from Atlantic to Pacific
without racism
without religious bigotry,
without overpopulation
and the destruction
of the natural world.

The Middle Continent
of the world,
this America,
existing long before
there was a United States
long before

a Dominion of Canada
long before
a Columbia.

We remember these things
and we shall
never forget
that this Pure Land, and its creatures,
have been
abused almost without remorse.

We can return
to America before the United States
only through our tears
through suffering
as we seek
to bring beauty behind us
beauty before us
once again.

Jack Forbes

January's Sun

The Sun appeared today
a welcome stranger
after three weeks of
dull grayness and cold,
storms and snow.

The light warms the room
streams past the plants
   in window boxes
touching my paper and
   my hands.

Sacred Sun
   precious light
a chemistry to lift my spirits
to quicken the beat
of my heart.

I was becoming
   a little crazy
restless with darkness
anxious and agitated
just yesterday
yearning for the light

And Today,
today it has come
   with blue skies
so rare here
so needed here.

I have tried, yes,
   I have tried to live
   in Northern land
   where fog and clouds
   deny the light.

And I have loved the greeness,
   the lushness of
   rain-nourished vegetation
   the hedgerows
   and grassy swells.

I have learned, indeed,
to cherish cloudy days
land to discover the
richness of colors
in shade,

but it is not enough!

Self-discovering, this winter,
more than ever before,
teaches me
how much
I need the Sun!

I tried two weeks in
Portugal
but December's Algarvian Sun
was not enough
and it was a month ago
you see.

So I sit by the window
today
in the Old Fire Station
Arts Centre Cafe
watching across George Street
the path of the Sun
as it traces
a southward arc
above Oxford's skyline.

A northward-facing cafe
will not do today!
I must have the Sun!
Wanishi, Gishux.

Nelson Augustine

Paradise Lost

John was sitting at the kitchen table having a coffee and looking out the window at the herd of cattle huddled at one end of the small field that was once the back yard of his quaint farmhouse. He missed tilling the soil. He regretted having to sell his tractors but it was either that or risk losing the farm when the bank foreclosed on his loan. John considered himself lucky that he still had his cattle; others had not fared so well. Since the floor dropped out on Wall Street, the dollar wasn't worth the paper it was printed on. The only problem was, he couldn't afford to buy hay and oats to feed his cattle. Already, the cattle had eaten their way through the five grazing pastures that surrounded his small farm. All that remained of these fields was a putrid concoction of mud and manure. John couldn't help but laugh at the absurdity of it all; he was robbing Peter in order to pay Paul. Even more bitter was another cliche, he was selling the farm. Why? Just so that he could hang on to a herd of dumb cattle.

Lance was making his way down toward the corner of the field near the forest. Big Bruce was already there as usual with his gang of domineering bulls. Lance was hungry and he doubted if Big Bruce would allow him to graze on the only patch of grass left growing in the field. Lance stopped and turned to look up at the farmhouse. That part of the herd which wasn't fortunate enough to belong to Big Bruce's exclusive club was up there already polishing off any tuft of grass that anybody else had overlooked. Lance decided to go up there anyway even if he knew that the pickings were slim. Rose and her calf were standing in the shade of the big oak tree with Molly and Fred.

"Big Bruce wouldn't let you join his club?" Rose asked Lance.

"Didn't even bother trying," replied Lance. "I wouldn't join them even if they begged me. Boys, am I hungry."

"Yeah, we're all hungry. There's nothing left except for that patch of grass Big Bruce and his gang are hoarding."

Fred, a young bull like Lance, suggested, "We should all get together and go down there and demand our share."

"What's the point'" Lance reminded them. "Once we finish off that patch, there'll be absolutely nothing left. We'll still be in the same predicament we're in now."

Molly, who had hadn't spoken since her calf took sick and died, was staring blankly off into the distance and commented to no one in particular, "I remember a time when the humans used to bring us oats and hay. Life was easy then. Yes, those were the good old days. Lance is right; the end is near."

Fred was painfully aware of his own growing hunger and frustrated over Big Bruce's monopolization of the only food source left. "Let's go down there anyway and wait until Big Bruce and the others go for some shade or water so we can at least get a little to eat for now."

"Big Bruce will just run us off anyway if we get too close," Rose cautioned.

"Not if we wait at the corner beside the forest. That way . . we'll be in a position to move in when Big Bruce leaves."

They had nothing to lose and agreed to wait beside the forest. They maneuvered into position under the suspicious glares of Big Bruce and his bulls. There was a group of deer eating sage in the forest on the other side of the fence. Lance had seen the deer there before but it had been months since they had last come around. Out of curiosity, Lance spoke to them.

"Hi there, it's been a while since you guys have been around. Where have you guys been?"

The stag who seemed to he the leader of the group answered, "The sage is especially delicious this time of year. We come by this way every year after we have eaten spring willow up on the ridge across the valley."

"I wouldn't mind having some sage right now," Lance wished aloud.

"You want some? I'll bring you some." The big stag picked a few sprigs with his teeth and brought them over to Lance.

"Thanks, friend. What's your name?"

"I am called Eagle Sees Him."

"Eagle Sees Him," Lance repeated. "What a peculiar name."

"An eagle was watching from a pine when I was born," Eagle Sees Him proudly proclaimed.

"Well, it's good to meet you, Eagle Sees Him. My name is Lance."

"Are the rest of your people hungry? My people can pick some sage and bring it to you. I see that there is nothing inside the fence."

"Indeed, and I would be deeply indebted to you."

And so the herd of deer brought sage for the hungry herd of cattle. The sage was far tastier than the grass and so it didn't take much of it to sate the cattle's appetite. Darkness began to fall and the deer retired to the forest in order to bed down. Lance and the rest of the segregated cattle watched with envy as the deer disappeared into the forest. Big Bruce watched all of this with curiosity but his greed would not permit him to abandon his patch of grass.

"If only this fence weren't here," Rose said. "Then we could eat wherever we pleased." Rose's statement spurred in Lance the memory of an event which had occurred earlier that spring. The herd had been pastured in a crude field that they had never grazed in before. The spot had obviously been part of the forest in the recent past. Old stumps and boulders littered the clearing. Lance remembered this field well because it was the debris strewn about it that caused him to stumble and fall through the fence. Lance was shaken but not hurt. The fence was demolished. Having related this memory to the others, Lance suggested that they knock down the fence. Lance turned to seek Fred's opinion but Fred was already charging the fence.

John had a bundle of boards under his arm as he tried to pick up the hammer. Robert, who had agreed to come over and help mend the fence, plucked the hammer off the ground and handed it to John. "Just the cows and young bulls are missing, huh? That's strange. Usually it's the old bulls that do the roaming."

"Well, I'm not going to lose anymore head. I'm taking these old bulls down to the slaughterhouse tomorrow. It's time to close up the shop. Darned animals done ate me out of house and home."

Patricia Bennett

Untitled

Walk with me
to purple skies
where the sun fades
and drops behind mountain
peaks

Snow flakes fall
erase the existence
disappear
on my tongue
as it searches
the open air
for something
not there

caught between the mountains
I climb to get out
only to grasp a handful
of light pink shale
steps taken
are forever long

I want to be home
the strings keep me
a struggle to be free
to run with wind
touch the plains
to see the sun set

Patricia Bennett

Untitled

Memories flow
It is the rain
cool and clear
heals and cleanses
my eyes search
the beauty
high above
the clouds
towards
the silent stars
that are stitched
and joined
beamed through
across the
darkened sky
whisps of white
and blue
drift thin strings
that now fade
but I will
remember
it was a clear
drop of rain

When A Grey Whale Sings to a Swan

When a grey whale sings to a swan,
A shrill cry leads a wisp of thought
Through the mist of an alley sky.
And a wolf screams at the south
Where warmth gleens snow crisp, white,
Blinding his eye.

An Inuit hunter drives a spear through a blowhole in ice
and catches tomorrow's food,
And the sea wolf swims
to the sea's depths of cold and dark,
minus one of her brood.

A whale bleeds at a propeller chop
Beneath the hull of a schooner ride.
Teens ride waves
And tots sculpture sand
As a cow drifts 'n with the tide.

A gull picks at a carcass
It's feathers ruffle as it swallows meat.
Upon a fire a crab screams
Into an echo chamber pot
Boiling water as cedar burns sweet.

A family drives home through forest and mountain,
Sea breeze trapped in the folds of a tent.
The gas they drive sucked through refinery
In a port from a half empty load
A tanker sent.

Another half remains in the sea, floating, breaking,
washing on rock and sand,
Globbing thick.
The lion turns black and dead birds bob
In sludge as crude turns sea sick.

Through the watch humans' eye,
air and sea die, and bird and whale are gone.
Through the wind and the rain,
The Haida feel the sea's pain,

and listen

as a grey whale sings to a swan.

Victoria Lena Manyarrows

In Spirit Together

another circle complete.

as the wind blows leaves and trees
into hundreds of swirls of color and sounds
and the heat rises from the earth
circling back in radiating patterns
of increasing warmth
through space
to the sun —

Drum Memory and Tonights Dream

like nights escaping from the sun
i run to you
fire burning, rivers surging
running to you to escape the heat
and seek out the cool, reassuring peace
of your arms

the drums pound out a memory
a memory of yesterday when our spirits
collided
shattering mountains
and everything between us
that was not the way i would have chosen to go
to go down warring, trembling
over misunderstandings and unsaid words
i wanted those waves to wash away those chains, those buried lies
i wanted those waves to let go of those pretenses
and remember those forgotten ways of saying i love you
with a smile and soft caress
waking
i feel you holding me soft
your arms a cradle calming me again
and bringing me back home to your ocean
your ever-rising waves of love
and compassion

Lorne Simon

Webs

Survival, when it is strictly only survival, is an ugly thing. Life is something more than just survival. To be alive is to know splendor and beauty. Living is an artform. I am immersed in art. I am forever spinning art from out of my flesh. My purpose in spinning webs is no longer merely to catch flies to eat. There is much more to it now. Indeed, the concern for food becomes incidental to the act of weaving a web. I love the feeling of being lost in abstractions for days at a time, recalculating the design of a work in progress with every shift in the breeze. Marvelous structures are woven and unwoven in my mind as I release filament and descend. Each web is a surprise, I myself never know what shape it will finally acquire. Every moment of creations is also a moment of re-creation, as the slightest changes in meteorology constantly alter and realign variables in physics and geometry. Supports, piers, brackets and braces demand existence in places that I had not imagined would require them. The weather alters everything.

The finished product, as I have already said is always a surprise. When I complete a web, I stand back into one of its corners and contemplate it, marvelling at the results of a genius that has spontaneously responded to every shift in the elements. I am not boasting. All spiders are possessed when engaged in the act of weaving. We enter a trance and dance with creation. The genius is never ours. We disappear from the world of appetite and enter into pure abstraction. It is never out of egotism that we marvel at our webs. We know that we were only instruments and that the web is a product of something much greater than ourselves.

I never like it when a fly lands on my work too soon after its completion. I need time to concentrate, on the undisturbed web. We believe that in contemplating webs the fullness of appreciation eventually blooms into realizations. Ideally, each web should yield a truth. But life being what it is - so full of chaos and so contrary to design - it is rare that any series of webs will yield their true potential to their creators. More likely than not a fly will crash into the web soon after its completion. How disturbing such moments are! How profoundly disturbing! On the one hand, there is the thrill of catching the next meal and, on the other hand, there is this extreme sense of violation as a part of oneself is rent to threads by the thrashings of a fly.

These moments are disturbing because they overwhelm us with those eternal questions. What is life, if it is not to be in the knowing of wonders? Why, then, does life interrupt itself? Why must the process of knowing be rudely dashed by matters of appetite? Why are not the worlds of appetite and abstraction in harmony? In other words, why does it so rarely happen that a web will remain undisturbed after its completion until it has yielded wisdom to the weaver? Ideally, a fly should land only after that golden moment. This happens by chance every now and again but it is really quite rare. Imagine how wise all arachnids could be!

Perhaps, however, we are not meant to know more than we should. There is a popular horror story told amongst us of a certain spider who once tried a most unusual experiment. He decided to construct three webs in a row. He planned to build the outside ones first and the inside one last. This way he figured the outside webs would shelter the inside one. The webs to the front and the back of the inside web would stop all the flies coming in from both directions. The central web would remain undisturbed and he could contemplate on this web for as long as he pleased. This he did. And when he had completed the project, he set himself on the corner of the inside web and observed. He studied the fascinating weave at his leisure. He sat there for hours and hours and great mysteries were gradually revealed to him. The wonders, however, that the web disclosed eventually trapped him just as surely as webs entangle flies.

He became totally consumed by the outpouring of knowing and he forgot himself. He forgot that he was a spider. He forgot that he had eight legs and a breast full of filament. All the knowing of himself vaporized. Just as he thought he was about to crack the riddle of the universe, a swallow came by and plucked him from his reveries.

I can never forget that story. And sometimes I can't help but think that webs are unnatural. If knowing can only come by fits end starts, then webs are illusions. This artform generates a false sense of completion and harmony. It deceptively suggests to us that it contains the all. In truth, knowing is not so neat and compartmental. Knowing is more like dew. It is everywhere, but it only gathers into little drops that plop off boughs one by one. Yet webs are not altogether deceptive. After all, they elevate the act of survival. Somehow webs prevent life from ever degenerating into ugliness.

Lorne Simon

Midst Poplar

To the rhythm of the salmon
Where they lie, flexing their gills
In pools, scraping their bellies
On pebbles, wagging their tails
In the deep cool Miramichi,
To this rhythm falls soft latin rain,
The tinkling of Spanish strings is
Heard everywhere
Sweet miserable notes wrung from
Ragged branches
Scuttle down dead aspen leaves,
Drip into pools...
Somewhere an old man softly remembers
Rosa and her hate feet,
I have come here midst poplar
To feel water soak through my feathers
And coo sad partridge words.

William George

The Seeds of Hope

The magic of life is in the beauty of nature
each pebble, each bark of cedar, each blade of grass
each wild rose, the forests, to the massive mountains
The purpose is to co-exist in harmony
Self interest shatters the bond in the life cycle
illusion is continually seeking eluding rewards
illusion is dangerous to our existence
illusion is detrimental to our survival
always taking and never giving back
draining our depleting resources
selfishness destroys unity and harmony
desolation will be our only consolation for greed
genuine deception happens when talking
in terms of greed and selfishness
passing off deception as something genuine
taking wild blackberries and replacing them with concrete
leaving roses bloodied
people are roses and our emotions are bloodied
try to harvest in our gardens
greed and selfishness are tractors
tearing up our gardens
greed and selfishness leave us bloodied roses
in barren gardens
We plant seeds of hope in the garden of life
seeds blossom into happiness
tractors cannot plough away the hope
when everything else is taken away
we plant seeds of hope
we again become one with the cedar, wild blackberries,
with ourselves, and with Mother Earth

Wayne Keon

earth walk talks

i heard
you took that long ride
out to clouds and sky and blue
heavens around you now
all finished with
this earth walk
it was a good one Tom
and I'm really glad
we met those times
coming in from around
all ends of this country
talking about the work we did
and sort of keeping
everyone straight on things
i can still see you talking
and smiling and talking
the earth walk talk
even here
at coquihalla
between clouds
and blue and shaman's mist
really needing
to be kept straight
and don't worry Tom
i'll be keeping
an eye on things
til I run into
you again
and remain
your friend
always
wayne

Wayne Keon

at allison pass

mountains
grow
along
the trail

and
climb

a slow sky
path
to
crow's nest
float and
drift

to eagle and raven

sail
through
clouds

turn and face the wind

and mist
haunt
me
likc
some shaman's
dream
rising
along side
these earthly trees
reaching for the peak

your voice and spirit
everywhere
now

if only i could
have you
here

but summits
wash
away

ascend
and
slowly

ascend
slowly
now

and
slowly
ascend
ascend
and rise
away

Sam Kewaquado

Dreams (Oratory)

The one very interesting phenomenon that I have not heard anyone talk about in this community is; speaking about their dreams, unless there was some debauchery connected with a particular dream or a forecast of something ominous. You know like in the days of old when the suspected bearwalkers told of ominous dreams of things to come, quite like our present day New Years predictions. If something happened, you wouldn't hear the end of it. Or on the other hand, if nothing happened there was no hoopla. Further to this I suspect some kind of mind control was evident. Anyway on to my story.

In this story I will name the Hunter "Neganbutoo" (He who runs ahead) as the third party to the revelation of my dream, which happened in mid-November of 1989.

As in all nights before I lay myself down to sleep I give thanks to my guardian spirit for the beautiful day had enjoyed whether the day was good or bad, asked for another day and planned the things I hoped to accomplish, bearing in mind that I should not ask for too much, for greed should not enter the picture.

As my mind followed the path into the dream-world I began to become familiar with my surroundings, the place I envisioned was a swamp road beyond a curve to a place where the deer gathered in late fall. There was snow on the ground and it was getting dark. Suddenly there was a flurry of movement and a deer was running away, I was not able to do anything. Then several shots rang out and the deer fell. I saw a body moving towards the dying deer and I was aware it was being dragged out to the road. One other thing I noticed was blood and a greenish substance seeping out the side of its' head, like an antler was missing.

When I awoke in the morning I said to my wife, "I had the most amazing dream last night," and I began to retell my wife.

It was after supper that same day "Neganbutoo" came over to visit and talk. During this lengthy conversation he began to speak of the night before..."He said you know I bought some cheap shells at a sale and of course they were no good, couldn't hit a barn door with them but seen a deer, actually a buck....." At that point I asked if I could interrupt him and asked my wife to recite the dream I had the night before. When the story was finished, "Neganbutoo" concluded his adventure by saying he fired several shots and he knew some did not make a hit, but one of the bullets hit the deer at the base of the antler and knocked it off. This explained why in my dream I saw blood and gore coming out of the deers' head.

I place a lot of emphasis on my dreams because the soul in my brain leaves in quest of knowledge from the after-world and in our own environment. And the soul in my heart had the nourishment for my body for another day. It was a good dream! Miigwetch.

Since my return to Shawanaga First Nation I have been involved in many short term projects and one of these jobs entailed doing research at our fish sanctuary on the mouth of the Shawanaga river.

During this month stay at the fish sanctuary, my cousin and I would go out every day and look for fuel wood. On one of these outings I found an old dead oak tree and began chopping off the branches and one of these branches I saw what resembled an ancient bird ready to take flight. I cut off the excess wood and took it back to base camp and showed my cousin. I recalled a story (legend) my father told me about our legendary culture hero "Nenbozhoo."

You see, this legendary hero "Nenbozhoo" had many capabilities and one of these capabilities was being able to transform himself into any creature or image he chose and what suited his situation.

This was one reason why I named this piece of wood after Nenbozhoo because it resembled a bird and the imagery became symbolic of this hero and often trickster, who caught the unwary because they did not heed his teachings.

The story my father told me goes something like this..

"Nenbozhoo was travelling the Great Lakes in search of his brother and as he was travelling up the eastern shores of Georgian Bay he came across some M'shibsheeg basking in the sun on a beach. As he came closer the M'shibsheeg escaped into the water and he could not shoot them with his bow and arrows. So he decided to wait for them to come to shore again but he also needed a place to hide so he would not be noticed. The only thing on the beach was an old stump of a tree, so wise old Nenbozhoo decided to wrap some of the bark of the tree around himself as a disguise. Sure enough the M'shibseeg returned to shore and all they saw was this old stump. Each of the M'shibsheeg asked of the stump and weren't sure so they asked three watersnakes which were coloured white, green, and black to go and check the stump. Each of these snakes wrapped themselves around this stump and tried with all their might to squeeze the stump but each time Nenbozhoo withstood their attempts to crush the stump. Satisfied, the M'shibsheeg came up on shore and slept. As they slept Nenbozhoo took his bow and arrows and shot them, but one escaped. The one that escaped caused the flooding of the land but that is another story. The birds told Nenbozhoo the M'shibsheeg killed his brother and this is why he sought to kill them. This is another reason why Ojibway people were able to live on this land was because they fasted when they went into the woods and the animals spoke to them and told the Ojibway how to live."

Sam Kewaquado

When I finished this story, I told my cousin I would name this piece after our culture hero. And Nenbozhoo would seek out the monies I needed to begin my dreams of a publishing company and help me with spreading the teaching of legends and the unification of Ojibway people on the shores of Georgian Bay.

Daniel David Moses

Her Moccasin Dream

Again the dream
of rain on the city,

of cold wet feet, old
moccasins. The dream

within that dream then,
the one of running

shoes, new and shite, comes
true but again for

only the moment
it takes to put food

to pavement. Then that
inner dream is gone

again with the rain
down the gutters and

that same old tanned worn
hide returns. This time,

though, those moccasins
contain an older

dream in which the sun
burns. So the dreams end

with laughter. Now you
walk on the water.

Daniel David Moses

Blues After Rain

A bit late in the day
for the rain to end. Out
over the lake, the break

up of clouds makes a lie
down for light. So it does,
as well it might, a yawn

or two of bright above
a town already blue
in its face with wet. Lie

down? You bet. Imagine
towers standing through storm
like trees, trying to scrape

the sky as we taught them.
What use standing up when
even the wind lies down

in the west and voices
of water insist on
rest? Lie down? Yes. Yes, yes.

D.L. Birchfield

River In A Tree

Upside-down as it can be
There's a river in a tree!
Rushing ever upward
From root to leaf it flows
Branching ever outward
It's up, up, up it goes
Pulled by the sun
Lifting water by the ton
From ground to tree to air
There's a river rushing there!
Flowing ever upward
Upward does it run
The air will be its ocean
In the clutches of the sun

Ryan Rice

Your Country

I am standing on the edge
but it is too far to see.
I know where it is
but I have not ties.
It's vast and beautiful,
lush and rugged,
familiar and unfamiliar.
So why are you here?
only to miss your mother.

(Song) "Last Stand"

(Dedicated to the Lubicon Cree)

Its said the meek shall inherit the Earth
But that day might be too late
the time has come for the meek to rise
the future of the children just won't wait.

CHORUS

We must make one last stand
shoulder to shoulder hand in hand
We are brothers of this land
We are sisters of this land

In the land of the Lubicon
the drum beats louder every day
The sound of wheels, the smell of oil
drove our brother the moose away

CHORUS

The promise land, you know the promise land
A promise made is a promise broken
Times are hard and they're only getting harder
Words are words forgotten as they're spoken
Chief Ominayak will lead our stand
stop the whitemans raping of the land

Chorus

KIDS

Sean Keon

Raven and Me

The raven is
a friend of mine.

He comes
to help
me
whenever
I need him.

He is always
close
to me

when
I miss
my dad.

He's always
there
when I need
him.

He comes
down
down
down
to see me
and my dad.

(Eight years old)

Rain

A pitter
a patter,
a sprinkle
a tinkle,
rumbling loud,
but soft.

Green-silver
stars glowing
in the night.

Dancing,
laughing,
talking,
running,
like rose petals
on your face.

(Eight years old)

Cherokee Blood-Rides-At-The-Door

Arctic Animal Countdown

Ten enormous musk oxes walking away wobbly.
Nine white ptarmigan eating on tree buds.
Eight baby caribou playing nicely on a patch of snow.
Seven fluffy snowy owls gliding quietly.
Six baby seals swimming all together.
Five fat narwhales fighting in the water.
Four arctic foxes going to get some bird eggs.
Three happy huskies running all day.
Two sad lemmings running away from caribou.
One jolly snowshoe hare jumping along.

Jenny Charlie

Sunsets

It goes a golden brown
a certain hour of everyday
you can see it from town
Even from the bay.
It is so nice and the colour
is just right.
Sometimes I wish it would stay
that golden light.

Jenny Charlie

Spring

SPRING
FLOWERS SUNNY
SHINING, GROWING, SPRINGING,
BRIGHTNESS, HAPPINESS, BLACKNESS, GLOOMINESS,
SNOWING, WHITENING, FALLING,
COLD, SNOW
WINTER

Mountains

Mountains

Gentle
as a cat
mountains roll

Tall
as the mountains surounding
mountains echo

Rivers

Strong
as a tornado
moves fast

Clear
as a spring
tumbling water

(Twelve years old)

GUESTS

(International Indigenous)

Marcos Parrado

An Offering of Appreciation to Mother Earth

In the night of the storm
Lightening struck a rock
And from a deep abyss
Was born a song
And it was man

The earth became flesh
And the heart of the earth
Began to beat strongly
Accompanying his song.

The musicians began to
Play hollow reeds
Like an echo
Which came from
newborn breath
And the heart of the earth
Beat in time with them

The earth began to
close once again
And the musicians began
To follow the path

Dawn arrived
along with the song
And it awoke the trees
Which moved their arms
As well as their legs
The rocks trembled
And their souls
were returned to them
All the flowers were born
Singing in chorus
with the musicians
Who were awakening
along the path

In the stream they came upon
Many sleeping men

who awoke and followed

When they arrived at the village
The others continued to sleep
Only a few awoke
And joined in the march
They left the people behind

The rest remained asleep
And their bodies
returned to stone
The songs were already
in the distance
They were returning
to the earth
And they took their souls

Time always brings Life
It seems like seeding time
but it's not
Even so it's very happy day
The dawn awoke smiling
The dew gathers together
her hair
And lets it loose
Playing in the breeze

The earth is happy
To open her bowels
And receive the seed of new life
And she is happier still today

When the blowing winds
Make everything sing in unison
Along the path
To the Old One
who is skipping
As he gives out the good news

Bewitched by the new life
The Old One moves haltingly
Without disrupting the harmony
And he continues
to deliver the news

The wind that is carrying
the Old One
Continues to bewitch everybody
Men gather along the road
The women
The clouds
New songs
The dust
And even the whole earth
The song is strong
That no one even if they
so desired
Could break away
from its charm

The sun begins to shine
Uniting everything
Her rays are playing
With the dew drops
The entire earth travels
With musical drops
of transparent rain
Which infiltrate the
perforated reeds.
While the wind plays tricks
Creating the music which flows
from reeds

The Old One steps forward
To become the most wise
And he demonstrates to all
The happy new life that
Today was born in the garden

Haunani-Kay Trask

I Go By the Moons

i go by the trail
of earth and green
sliver of sun
pendulous rain

i go by the dream trees
flame trees hissing
and swaying

i go by the shores
and coconut dunes, soft crab
sand in my heart

i go by the temples
maile vines fresh
with tears

i go by the taro
velvet-leafed god
flesh and mud

i go by the thrust
of Kōnāhuanui
his lava jet
jewelled with fern

i go by the moons
expectant
feeling in the throat
for the chanter

maile: a fragrant vine used by Hawaiians for wreaths and altar decoration.

Ko'olauloa

          i ride those ridge backs
down each narrow
cliff   red hills
          and bird song in my
head   gold dust
on my face   nothing

whispers but the trees
          mountains blue beyond
my sight   pools of
icy water at my feet

          this earth glows the color
of my skin   sunburnt
natives didn't fly

          from far away
but sprouted whole through
velvet   taro   in the sweet mud

of this 'âina
their ancient name
is kept   my piko
safely sleeps

          famous rains
flood down
in tears

i know these hills
my lovers   chant them

late at night

owls swoop
          to touch me:

'aumâkua

NOTE:

Ko'olauloa-long Ko'olau - is the district on the windward side of the island of O'ahu that stretches from Kane'obe to La'ie. The Ko'olau mountain range is characterized by razor-backed ridges, lush with vegetation, that display dozens of waterfalls and heavy rains. These mountains are the oldest in the Hawaiian islands, having deep valleys at their base, meandering rivers once teeming with fish and shellfish, and several wetlands in which our ancestors cultivated taro.

Throughout Polynesia, the piko-navel cord - is buried or secreted away after birth because of its sacred connection to life. Where the piko is buried determined part of the Hawaiian identification with home, or birthplace.

The 'aumâkua - ancestral god - is a family god, in animal form, that protects those who claim it. 'Aumâkua are passed down through generations and require protection from their descendants. The Hawaiian owl - pueo - is considered by some members of my family to be an 'aumâkua to us

'aina — land that feeds

taro — the Hawaiian staple from which poi - a thick, delicious paste, is make.

Blood on the Land

mourning floods the 'aina
quiet oil of green
yellowing
la'i leaves

'awapubi
crumbling at the root
lizard skeletons wildly
strewn

how the sun slits
the air niu and ulu
dying against
pure mountin blue

a stronger light
from great seams of Ko'olau
not desperate
long and clear

falling with the flight
of 'iwa

below pesticidal
waterlands lazily
killing
sinister glare
off a smoking sea

and black
illuminations
as trees

'aina	land that feeds
la'i	ti leaves
'awapuhi	fragrant ginger
nui	coconut
ulu	breadfruit
Ko'olau	the lush, razor-backed mountain range that divides the island of O'ahu into Windward and Leeward districts
'iwa	frigate bird

ELDERS

Lavina White (Haida Nation)

Roots and Wings

There is nothing more that we parents can do than give our children roots and wings. We teach them all we can at home and the rest is entirely up to them to figure out.

One time when one of my sons was a child he said to me, "Mom, I think I know why they are taking down our forests and our totem poles, and disturbing our graves." And I said, "Why?" And he said, "So that we won't be able to tell that these are our homelands".

Back home we people of the Haida Nation have started calling our sacred islands 'Haida-Gwai', because that's what we always called them. We don't call them 'Queen Charlotte Islands' anymore, because that's what the whiteman called them. And so I urge all our First Nations to re-establish our own names for our homelands. Each of us has our own names for our mountains, our valleys, our lakes, and rivers. Re-establish those names! Then we will always be reminded that those are our homelands, and that the Creator gave us the responsibility of looking after those homelands and governing ourselves in our own home.

The Creator did not put us here so that we would have to be subservient to somebody else's provincial or federal government, or somebody else's rules. We don't fit into their governments and their laws and their ways, because many of their values are in direct conflict with ours. And so our First Nations must re-establish our own distinct governments too. That is the only way that there is hope for our people and our land.

Glen Douglas (Okanagan Nation)

This Sacred Land

The land on which we live is sacred. I know this because many many Native people lived here in Peace and Harmony with the Nature Spirits. The people did not have policemen, padlocks, prisons, penitentiaries, or burglar alarms. Nor did they have the "book" (the Bible). But they knew about the Great Spirit, who created everything.

A great chief of the Similaka-meugh (Eagle People, now known as Similkameen) was born in this place, along with others of the People, before and after him. They all drank the crystal clear water of the valley's rivers and streams, grew their food on its unpoisoned soil, breathed its fresh, clean air, and worshipped the power of the Sun as it blessed them with life each morning.

Our Ancestors had a special respect for the Mother Earth and all it offered them. I'm told by Elders they built their shelters in the ground, which provided them with an insulated warmth in the winter and a cool dwelling in the summer. If one looks carefully around this area, one can see signs of this lifestyle.

Many of the valley People respected the wild creatures which walked the land, flew in its winds, and swam in its rivers. They took only that which they truly needed for food and gave thanks to the Creator for those provisions. Life was much less complex then, and the People of "The Ashnola, Similkameen and Okanagan Valleys" enjoyed life that way.

It makes my heart heavy when I see our Native people forgetting the true and good ways of our ancestors. It saddens me to see them come in with bulldozers, drive over, scrape off, and flatten out our sacred Mother Earth which housed, fed, and buried the People. It is unfortunate to see the Red Man, slowly becoming a "brown" white man as he puts the value of money and material possessions above his oneness with the spirit in all living things. He has forgotten that Grandfather Sun, Mother Earth, Grandmother Moon and our Spirited Waters need to be honored, respected, cared for, and shared with for their Spiritual, Emotional, Mental, and Physical powers. He has forgotten that those powers also lie within himself, waiting to be revealed and united with others in a positive way.

When a child does something very wrong, a good parent will take away a special privilege which the child is used to. When the child shows that he has learned something positive by making his mistake, then he is allowed to regain the privilege.

If we, the children of this land do not show more honor, respect, caring, and sharing for the special privilege of living on this - The Mother Earth - then she and Grandfather Sun, through the power of the Great Spirit, may take away this great privilege which we have selfishly taken for granted. This great reward is called "Life." It is experienced by showing Love and Respect for all natural elements - earth, air, fire, water, wind, and for wildlife and all living things on which Human Beings are dependent, remember. Let us remember that the way to live in peace and harmony with each other and our surroundings is to be at peace with ourselves. Many of the things which have tempted Red and White men alike have made him seemingly very unloving and unpeaceful. May we overcome all those qualities we do not need (such as greed), by showing the Good Qualities of our True Nature — like "Giving". Most importantly, may we know and remember that we have, deep within our beings - a Peaceful and Loving Spirit. It is time to let it out!

May we remember these truths as life, here - in this valley, in other valleys, and on this Planet depends on us knowing and living them.

We can choose to learn from our Traditional and Spiritual elders to live in harmony and balance with all things. Or, we can choose to learn from those who seek to profit, no matter what the cost to Mother Earth. If it is to survive - the natural world, the world we all know and love - needs protection and understanding. *IF IT DOES NOT SURVIVE, OF COURSE, NEITHER WILL WE!!!!*

AUTHOR BIOGRAPHIES

BIOGRAPHIES

Bennett, Patricia

A Saulteaux from Manitoba, she is a graduate of The En'owkin International School of Writing who currently lives in Calgary.

Blood-Rides-At-The-Door, Cherokee

An eight year old Blackfoot girl who currently lives on the Blood Reserve in Alberta.

Bonneau, Tracey Kim

Okanagan from the Penticton Indian Band. She has been free-lance producing 1/2 hour T.V. programs for the talk show Kla-How-Ya (15 year Native Program) . Her future plans are to become an Independent Producer to produce a feature film.

Brant, Jamieson C.

Mohawk (with Delaware and Irish lineage) from the Six Nations Reserve in Southern Ontario. She is currently working as Coordinator of a Native Language Teaching Materials Database for the Native Cultural Centres in Ontario.

Crank, Dan L.

From the Navajo Tribe and belongs to the Bitahni and Kinlichini clan. He is currently living on the Navajo Reservation and working as an educator with Navajo School Districts. Born in Dennechotso (Green Meadows), he remains traditional in the Navajo Community.

Cross, Neil

Mohawk from Kahnawake. Student at the Kahnawake Survival School.

Damm, Kateri

Ojibway from Cape Croker Reserve in Ontario, she is a vice-president of the Aboriginal Youth Council of Canada, currently completing her Masters Degree in Literature at University of Ottawa.

Dandurand, Joseph A.

From the Sto:Lo Nation in BC, he is currently living in Ottawa studying at University of Ottawa.

DeBassige, Mary Lou C.

Odawa, Ojibway and Scottish descent from West Bay First Nation on Manitoulin Island, Ontario, she is currently studying at The En'owkin International School of Writing.

Eagle Tail-Feathers, Shirley

Blackfoot/Sioux/Saulteaux, she is presently studying anthropology at University of Regina in Saskatchewan.

Forbes, Jack

Director of Native American Studies at the University of California, his tribal affiliations are Delaware-Lenpa and Powhantan-Renape. His latest book is entitled "Columbus and Cannibals".

Garner, Judi

A First Nations women living in Beverdell, BC. She is currently writing a series of childrens' books entitled "When the Earth Was Young".

George, William

Salish from the Burrard Reserve near Vancouver, William is nephew of the late Chief Dan George. He is currently a student at the En'owkin International School of Writing.

Hammerton, Leona

A member of the Shuswap Nation, she is a graduate of The En'owkin International School of Writing.

Keon, Sean

An 8 year old Ojibway currently living in Toronto.

Keon, Wayne

A member of the Ojibway Nation, he is a well known author of Native literature and poetry. A business administration graduate, he is also a painter and financial analyst.

Kewaquado, Samuel

An Ojibway traditionalist from Shawanaga First Nation. He published an Ojibway/English colouring book in 1989.

Lawrence, Mary

An Okanagan from the Westbank Indian Band in BC, she is currently enrolled at The En'owkin International School of Writing. She recently published her first book of poetry entitled "In Spirit and Song".

Louie, Arnold

From the Okanagan Nation, he is enroled in The En'owkin International School of Writing and also working for The Osoyoos Indian Band.

Manossa, Geraldine

Cree from Bigstone Band in Northern Alberta, she is a graduate of the Native Theatre School of Toronto and The En'owkin International School of Writing.

Maracle, Lee

A renowned author of Cree and Salish ancestry, she has written several books including "Bobbi Lee; Indian Rebel", "I Am Woman" and her latest, "Sundogs". She is also a former instructor at The En'owkin International School of Writing.

Marchand, Duane E.

An Okanagan from the Vernon Reserve in B.C. He is a former student of the En'owkin International School of Writing. He is currently a reporter for the Senklip News for the Okanagan Indian Band. His writing has also appeared in the Province Newspaper and Kahtou both located in Vancouver B.C.

Mojica, Monique

A Kuna/Rappahannock woman word warrior, a mother, and an actress. Born in New York City, she came to Canada as a founding member of Native Earth Performing Arts and is a former Artistic Director of that company. She is also the Associate Director of the Native Theatre School.

Montour, Joel

From the Mohawk Nation and is currently a student at Kahnawake Survival School in Quebec. He is 16 years old.

Moses, Daniel David

A Delaware poet and Playwright from the Six Nations lands on the Grand River in Southern Ontario. His publications include the play Coyote City (Williams and Wallace 1990), the book of poems The White Line (fifth house 1990) and was the co-editor for : AN ANTHOGOGY OF CANADIAN NATIVE LITERATURE IN ENGLISH (Oxford 1992).

Mountain, Antoine

From the Dene Nation in the North West Territories. He is a visual artist as well as a writer. He attended Art School in Toronto from 1978 - 82.

Oandasan, William

A Tan'om (Slope people) of the Ukomn'om (Valley People) at the Round Valley reserve in Northern California. Round Valley Songs, his thesis for the Master of Fine Arts degree in creative writing, won an American Book Award. His Poetry also appears in Harpers Anthology of 20th Century Native American Poetry.

O'Sullivan, Gunargie

From the Kwagiuth Nation in Alert Bay, BC, currently residing in Vancouver. She is an actress who latest part was in a production of Thompson Highway's "Rez Sisters". She is currently working as co-producer of the film "The Enduring Potlach".

Paul-Martin, Michael

A Cree from James Bay in Northern Quebec, he is a former Trent University Native Studies student and currently enrolled at The En'owkin International School of Writing.

Peal, Charmaine

A young Nisgaa' woman from New Aiyansh. Her Indian name is "Naxnokgumgannaw" and she is of the Raven Clan. She is a student attending the En'owkin International School of Writing.

Porter, Murray

Oneida from the Six Nations on the Grand River. Murray has been a musician, singer and songwriter for 15 years. He spent many years playing with the BAR ROAD BAND and during those years had opportunity to play with BO DIDDLY, MATT MINGLEWOOD AND DAVID WILCOX.

Ruffo, Garnet

Ojibway from Northern Ontario, and graduate of Writing Program at Banff Centre School of Fine Arts, he holds an Honours Degree in English Literature at University of Ottawa.

Sanderson, Sheila

A Cree from The Pas, Manitoba, she is a former researcher for Manitoba Museum of Man now completing a degree program at University of Winnipeg.

Shisheesh, Angela

Cree from the Attawapiskat Reserve on the West coast of James Bay, Ontario. She is currently working at the Ojibway-Cree Cultural Centre in Timmins, Ontario as the Literacy Coordinator.

Taylor, Drew

A successful Ojibway script writer and playwright now residing in Toronto.

Van Camp, Richard

From the Dene Nation in the North West Territories. He is a student at the En'owkin International School of Writing.

Volbroth, Judith Mountain-Leaf

Born in the Moon of Changing Leaves in New York City, she is member of the Commanche Nation. She is also author of "Thunder Root: Traditional and Contemporary Native American Verse".

Wasegijig, Jean

An Odawa, freelance writer, poet, editor from the Wekwemikong Reserve in central Ontario. After graduating from Douglas College in New Westminster, B.C. with a diploma in Applied Arts, she went on to complete her third year at Simon Fraser University, Burnaby, B.C.,and majored in psychology.

Welburn, Ron

Cherokee-Conoy residing in Hadley , MA. U.S.A. He is currently teaching in the English department at U Mass-Amherst. He offered his first Native Literature course in the summer of 1992.

Wheeeler, Jordan

Cree author of "Brothers in Arms", he is presently living in Calgary finishing a new novel and writing for CBC.

William, Cody

12 years old, he is Chilcotin/Shuswap from the Williams Lake Indian Band, Sugar Cane Reserve, in B.C. He has also been Grass Dancing at Pow-Wows since he was 5 years old.

Williams, Muriel

From the Gitksan Nation she is currently residing in Vancouver where she is taking a creative writing course at Carnegie Community Centre

Young-Ing, Greg

Cree from The Pas, Manitoba, currently working at The En'owkin Centre.